W9-BBI-588

THE VOYAGE
OF THE
DAWN TREADER

C. S. Lewis.

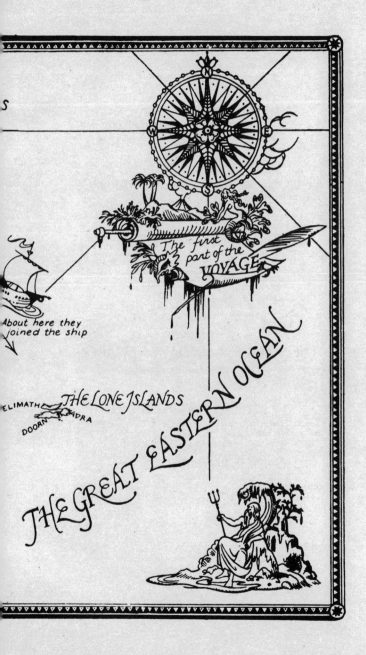

S

The first part of the VOYAGE

About here they joined the ship

ELIMATH   THE LONE ISLANDS
DOORN   AVRA

THE GREAT EASTERN OCEAN

Book One
THE MAGICIAN'S NEPHEW

Book Two
THE LION, THE WITCH AND THE WARDROBE

Book Three
THE HORSE AND HIS BOY

Book Four
PRINCE CASPIAN

Book Five
THE VOYAGE OF THE DAWN TREADER

Book Six
THE SILVER CHAIR

Book Seven
THE LAST BATTLE

C. S. LEWIS

Book Five

THE VOYAGE
OF THE
DAWN TREADER

Illustrated by PAULINE BAYNES

HARPER
An Imprint of HarperCollinsPublishers

NARNIA®

Although *The Magician's Nephew* was written several years after C. S. Lewis first began THE CHRONICLES OF NARNIA®, he wanted it to be read as the first book in the series. HarperCollins is happy to present these books in the order in which Professor Lewis preferred.

The Chronicles of Narnia®, Narnia® and all book titles, characters and locales original to The Chronicles of Narnia are trademarks of C.S. Lewis Pte. Ltd. Use without permission is strictly prohibited.

The Voyage of the *Dawn Treader*
Copyright © 1952 by C.S. Lewis Pte. Ltd.
Copyright renewed 1980 by C.S. Lewis Pte. Ltd.
Interior art by Pauline Baynes; copyright © 1952 by C.S. Lewis Pte. Ltd.
All rights reserved. No part of this book may be used or reproduced in any manner whatsoever without written permission except in the case of brief quotations embodied in critical articles and reviews.
Printed in the United States of America. For information address HarperCollins Children's Books, a division of HarperCollins Publishers, 10 East 53rd Street, New York, NY 10022.
www.narnia.com

Library of Congress Cataloging-in-Publication Data
Lewis, C. S. (Clive Staples), 1898–1963
  The voyage of the Dawn Treader / C. S. Lewis ; illustrated by Pauline
Baynes.
    p. cm. — (The Chronicles of Narnia ; bk 5)
  Summary: Lucy and Edmund, accompanied by their peevish cousin Eustace,
sail to the land of Narnia where Eustace is temporarily transformed into a
green dragon because of his selfish behavior and skepticism.
  ISBN 978-0-06-200841-1
  [1. Fantasy.] I. Baynes, Pauline, ill. II. Title. III. Series: Lewis, C.S. (Clive
Staples), 1898–1963. Chronicles of Narnia (HarperCollins (Firm)) ; bk 5.
PZ7.L58474Vo 1994   93-11515
[Fic]—dc20   CIP
                                                                                 AC

10 11 12 13 14   LP/CW   10 9 8 7 6 5 4 3 2 1

To Geoffrey Barfield

CONTENTS

THE PICTURE
IN THE BEDROOM

THERE WAS A BOY CALLED EUSTACE
Clarence Scrubb, and he almost deserved it. His
parents called him Eustace Clarence and masters
called him Scrubb. I can't tell you how his friends
spoke to him, for he had none. He didn't call his
Father and Mother "Father" and "Mother," but
Harold and Alberta. They were very up-to-date
and advanced people. They were vegetarians, non-
smokers and teetotalers and wore a special kind of
underclothes. In their house there was very little
furniture and very few clothes on beds and the
windows were always open.

Eustace Clarence liked animals, especially bee-
tles, if they were dead and pinned on a card. He
liked books if they were books of information and
had pictures of grain elevators or of fat foreign
children doing exercises in model schools.

Eustace Clarence disliked his cousins the four
Pevensies, Peter, Susan, Edmund and Lucy. But he

was quite glad when he heard that Edmund and
Lucy were coming to stay. For deep down inside
him he liked bossing and bullying; and, though he
was a puny little person who couldn't have stood
up even to Lucy, let alone Edmund, in a fight, he
knew that there are dozens of ways to give people
a bad time if you are in your own home and they
are only visitors.

Edmund and Lucy did not at all want to come
and stay with Uncle Harold and Aunt Alberta. But
it really couldn't be helped. Father had got a job
lecturing in America for sixteen weeks that summer, and Mother was to go with him because she
hadn't had a real holiday for ten years. Peter was
working very hard for an exam and he was to
spend the holidays being coached by old Professor
Kirke in whose house these four children had had

wonderful adventures long ago in the war years. If he had still been in that house he would have had them all to stay. But he had somehow become poor since the old days and was living in a small cottage with only one bedroom to spare. It would have cost too much money to take the other three all to America, and Susan had gone.

Grown-ups thought her the pretty one of the family and she was no good at school work (though otherwise very old for her age) and Mother said she "would get far more out of a trip to America than the youngsters." Edmund and Lucy tried not to grudge Susan her luck, but it was dreadful having to spend the summer holidays at their Aunt's. "But it's far worse for me," said Edmund, "because you'll at least have a room of your own and I shall have to share a bedroom with that record stinker, Eustace."

The story begins on an afternoon when Edmund and Lucy were stealing a few precious minutes alone together. And of course they were talking about Narnia, which was the name of their own private and secret country. Most of us, I suppose, have a secret country but for most of us it is only an imaginary country. Edmund and Lucy were luckier than other people in that respect. Their secret country was real. They had already visited it twice; not in a game or a dream but in reality. They had got there of course by Magic, which is the only way of getting to Narnia. And a promise, or very nearly a promise, had been made them in Narnia itself that they would some day get back. You may imagine that they talked about it a good deal, when they got the chance.

They were in Lucy's room, sitting on the edge of her bed and looking at a picture on the opposite wall. It was the only picture in the house that they liked. Aunt Alberta didn't like it at all (that was why it was put away in a little back room upstairs), but she couldn't get rid of it because it had been a wedding present from someone she did not want to offend.

It was a picture of a ship—a ship sailing straight toward you. Her prow was gilded and shaped like the head of a dragon with wide-open mouth. She had only one mast and one large, square sail which was a rich purple. The sides of the ship—what you could see of them where the gilded wings of the dragon ended—were green. She had just run up to the top of one glorious blue wave, and the nearer slope of that wave came down toward you, with streaks and bubbles on it. She was obviously running fast before a gay wind, listing over a little on her port side. (By the way, if you are going to read this story at all, and if you don't know already, you had better get it into your head that the left of a ship when you are looking ahead, is *port*, and the right is *starboard*.) All the sunlight fell on her from that side, and the water on that side was full of greens and purples. On the other, it was darker blue from the shadow of the ship.

"The question is," said Edmund, "whether it doesn't make things worse, *looking* at a Narnian ship when you can't get there."

"Even looking is better than nothing," said Lucy. "And she is such a very Narnian ship."

"Still playing your old game?" said Eustace Clarence, who had been listening outside the door and now came grinning into the room. Last year, when he had been staying with the Pevensies, he had managed to hear them all talking of Narnia and he loved teasing them about it. He thought of course that they were making it all up; and as he was far too stupid to make anything up himself, he did not approve of that.

"You're not wanted here," said Edmund curtly.

"I'm trying to think of a limerick," said Eustace. "Something like this:

"Some kids who played games about Narnia
Got gradually balmier and balmier—"

"Well *Narnia* and *balmier* don't rhyme, to begin with," said Lucy.

"It's an assonance," said Eustace.

"Don't ask him what an assy-thingummy is,"

said Edmund. "He's only longing to be asked. Say nothing and perhaps he'll go away."

Most boys, on meeting a reception like this, would either have cleared out or flared up. Eustace did neither. He just hung about grinning, and presently began talking again.

"Do you like that picture?" he asked.

"For heaven's sake don't let him get started about Art and all that," said Edmund hurriedly, but Lucy, who was very truthful, had already said, "Yes, I do. I like it very much."

"It's a rotten picture," said Eustace.

"You won't see it if you step outside," said Edmund.

"Why do you like it?" said Eustace to Lucy.

"Well, for one thing," said Lucy, "I like it because the ship looks as if it was really moving. And the water looks as if it was really wet. And the waves look as if they were really going up and down."

Of course Eustace knew lots of answers to this, but he didn't say anything. The reason was that at that very moment he looked at the waves and saw that they did look very much indeed as if they were going up and down. He had only once been in a ship (and then only as far as the Isle of Wight) and had been horribly seasick. The look of the waves in the picture made him feel sick again. He turned rather green and tried another look.

And then all three children were staring with open mouths.

What they were seeing may be hard to believe when you read it in print, but it was almost as hard to believe when you saw it happening. The things in the picture were moving. It didn't look at all like a cinema either; the colors were too real and clean and out-of-doors for that. Down went the prow of the ship into the wave and up went a great shock of spray. And then up went the wave behind her, and her stern and her deck became visible for the first time, and then disappeared as the next wave came to meet her and her bows went up again. At the same moment an exercise book which had been lying beside Edmund on the bed flapped, rose and sailed through the air to the wall behind him, and Lucy felt all her hair whipping round her face as it does on a windy day. And this was a windy day; but the wind was blowing out of the picture toward them. And suddenly with the wind came the noises—the swishing of waves and the slap of water against the ship's sides and the creaking and the over-all high steady roar of air and water. But it was the smell, the wild, briny smell, which really convinced Lucy that she was not dreaming.

"Stop it," came Eustace's voice, squeaky with fright and bad temper. "It's some silly trick you two are playing. Stop it. I'll tell Alberta—Ow!"

The other two were much more accustomed to adventures, but, just exactly as Eustace Clarence said "Ow," they both said "Ow" too. The reason was that a great cold, salt splash had broken right out of the frame and they were breathless from the smack of it, besides being wet through.

"I'll smash the rotten thing," cried Eustace; and then several things happened at the same time. Eustace rushed toward the picture. Edmund, who knew something about magic, sprang after him, warning him to look out and not to be a fool. Lucy grabbed at him from the other side and was dragged forward. And by this time either they had grown much smaller or the picture had grown bigger. Eustace jumped to try to pull it off the wall and found himself standing on the frame; in front of him was not glass but real sea, and wind and waves rushing up to the frame as they might to a rock. He lost his head and clutched at the other two who had jumped up beside him. There was a second of struggling and shouting, and just as they thought they had got their balance a great blue roller surged up round them, swept them off their feet, and drew them down into the sea. Eustace's despairing cry suddenly ended as the water got into his mouth.

Lucy thanked her stars that she had worked hard at her swimming last summer term. It is true that she would have got on much better if she had

used a slower stroke, and also that the water felt a great deal colder than it had looked while it was only a picture. Still, she kept her head and kicked her shoes off, as everyone ought to do who falls into deep water in their clothes. She even kept her mouth shut and her eyes open. They were still quite near the ship; she saw its green side towering high above them, and people looking at her from the deck. Then, as one might have expected, Eustace clutched at her in a panic and down they both went.

When they came up again she saw a white figure diving off the ship's side. Edmund was close beside her now, treading water, and had caught the arms of the howling Eustace. Then someone else, whose face was vaguely familiar, slipped an arm under her from the other side. There was a lot of shouting going on from the ship, heads crowding together above the bulwarks, ropes being thrown. Edmund and the stranger were fastening ropes round her. After that followed what seemed a very long delay during which her face got blue and her teeth began chattering. In reality the delay was not very long; they were waiting till the moment when she could be got on board the ship without being dashed against its side. Even with all their best endeavors she had a bruised knee when she finally stood, dripping and shivering, on the deck. After her Edmund was heaved up, and then the

miserable Eustace. Last of all came the stranger—
a golden-headed boy some years older than herself.

"Ca—Ca—Caspian!" gasped Lucy as soon as
she had breath enough. For Caspian it was;
Caspian, the boy king of Narnia whom they had
helped to set on the throne during their last visit.
Immediately Edmund recognized him too. All
three shook hands and clapped one another on the
back with great delight.

"But who is your friend?" said Caspian almost
at once, turning to Eustace with his cheerful smile.
But Eustace was crying much harder than any boy
of his age has a right to cry when nothing worse
than a wetting has happened to him, and would
only yell out, "Let me go. Let me go back. I don't
like it."

"Let you go?" said Caspian. "But where?"

Eustace rushed to the ship's side, as if he expected to see the picture frame hanging above the

sea, and perhaps a glimpse of Lucy's bedroom. What he saw was blue waves flecked with foam, and paler blue sky, both spreading without a break to the horizon. Perhaps we can hardly blame him if his heart sank. He was promptly sick.

"Hey! Rynelf," said Caspian to one of the sailors. "Bring spiced wine for their Majesties. You'll need something to warm you after that dip." He called Edmund and Lucy their Majesties because they and Peter and Susan had all been Kings and Queens of Narnia long before his time. Narnian time flows differently from ours. If you spent a hundred years in Narnia, you would still come back to our world at the very same hour of the very same day on which you left. And then, if you went back to Narnia after spending a week here, you might find that a thousand Narnian years had passed, or only a day, or no time at all. You never know till you get there. Consequently, when the Pevensie children had returned to Narnia last time for their second visit, it was (for the Narnians) as if King Arthur came back to Britain, as some people say he will. And I say the sooner the better.

Rynelf returned with the spiced wine steaming in a flagon and four silver cups. It was just what one wanted, and as Lucy and Edmund sipped it they could feel the warmth going right down to their toes. But Eustace made faces and spluttered and spat it out and was sick again and began to cry again and asked if they hadn't any Plumptree's Vitaminized Nerve Food and could it be made with distilled water and anyway he insisted on being put ashore at the next station.

"This is a merry shipmate you've brought us, Brother," whispered Caspian to Edmund with a chuckle; but before he could say anything more Eustace burst out again.

"Oh! Ugh! What on earth's *that*! Take it away, the horrid thing."

He really had some excuse this time for feeling a little surprised. Something very curious indeed had come out of the cabin in the poop and was slowly approaching them. You might call it—and indeed it was—a Mouse. But then it was a Mouse on its hind legs and stood about two feet high. A thin band of gold passed round its head under one ear and over the other and in this was stuck a long crimson feather. (As the Mouse's fur was very dark, almost black, the effect was bold and striking.) Its left paw rested on the hilt of a sword very nearly as long as its tail. Its balance, as it paced gravely along the swaying deck, was perfect, and its manners courtly. Lucy and Edmund recognized it at once—Reepicheep, the most valiant of all the Talking Beasts of Narnia, and the Chief Mouse. It had won undying glory in the second Battle of Beruna. Lucy longed, as she had always done, to take Reepicheep up in her arms and cuddle him.

But this, as she well knew, was a pleasure she could never have: it would have offended him deeply. Instead, she went down on one knee to talk to him.

Reepicheep put forward his left leg, drew back his right, bowed, kissed her hand, straightened himself, twirled his whiskers, and said in his shrill, piping voice:

"My humble duty to your Majesty. And to King Edmund, too." (Here he bowed again.) "Nothing except your Majesties' presence was lacking to this glorious venture."

"Ugh, take it away," wailed Eustace. "I hate mice. And I never could bear performing animals. They're silly and vulgar and—and sentimental."

"Am I to understand," said Reepicheep to Lucy after a long stare at Eustace, "that this singularly discourteous person is under your Majesty's protection? Because, if not—"

At this moment Lucy and Edmund both sneezed.

"What a fool I am to keep you all standing here in your wet things," said Caspian. "Come on below and get changed. I'll give you my cabin of course, Lucy, but I'm afraid we have no women's clothes on board. You'll have to make do with some of mine. Lead the way, Reepicheep, like a good fellow."

"To the convenience of a lady," said Reepicheep, "even a question of honor must give way—at least for the moment—" and here he looked very hard at Eustace. But Caspian hustled them on and in a few minutes Lucy found herself passing through the door into the stern cabin. She fell in love with it at once—the three square windows that looked out on the blue, swirling water astern, the low cushioned benches round three sides of the table, the swinging silver lamp overhead (Dwarfs' work, she knew at once by its exquisite delicacy) and the flat gold image of Aslan the Lion on the forward wall above the door. All this she took in in a flash, for Caspian immediately opened a door on the starboard side, and said, "This'll be your room, Lucy. I'll just get some dry things for myself"—he was rummaging in one of the lockers while he spoke—"and then leave you to change. If you'll fling your wet things outside the door I'll get them taken to the galley to be dried."

Lucy found herself as much at home as if she had been in Caspian's cabin for weeks, and the motion of the ship did not worry her, for in the old days when she had been a queen in Narnia she had done a good deal of voyaging. The cabin was very tiny but bright with painted panels (all birds and beasts and crimson dragons and vines) and spotlessly clean. Caspian's clothes were too big for her, but she could manage. His shoes, sandals and sea-boots were hopelessly big but she did not mind going barefoot on board ship. When she had finished dressing she looked out of her window at the water rushing past and took a long deep breath. She felt quite sure they were in for a lovely time.

ON BOARD
THE *DAWN TREADER*

"AH, THERE YOU ARE, LUCY," SAID Caspian. "We were just waiting for you. This is my captain, the Lord Drinian."

A dark-haired man went down on one knee and kissed her hand. The only others present were Reepicheep and Edmund.

"Where is Eustace?" asked Lucy.

"In bed," said Edmund, "and I don't think we can do anything for him. It only makes him worse if you try to be nice to him."

"Meanwhile," said Caspian, "we want to talk."

"By Jove, we do," said Edmund. "And first, about time. It's a year ago by our time since we left you just before your coronation. How long has it been in Narnia?"

"Exactly three years," said Caspian.

"All going well?" asked Edmund.

"You don't suppose I'd have left my kingdom and put to sea unless all was well," answered the

King. "It couldn't be better. There's no trouble at all now between Telmarines, Dwarfs, Talking Beasts, Fauns and the rest. And we gave those troublesome giants on the frontier such a good beating last summer that they pay us tribute now. And I had an excellent person to leave as Regent while I'm away—Trumpkin, the Dwarf. You remember him?"

"Dear Trumpkin," said Lucy, "of course I do. You couldn't have made a better choice."

"Loyal as a badger, Ma'am, and valiant as—as a Mouse," said Drinian. He had been going to say "as a lion" but had noticed Reepicheep's eyes fixed on him.

"And where are we heading for?" asked Edmund.

"Well," said Caspian, "that's rather a long story. Perhaps you remember that when I was a child my usurping uncle Miraz got rid of seven friends of my father's (who might have taken my part) by sending them off to explore the unknown Eastern Seas beyond the Lone Islands."

"Yes," said Lucy, "and none of them ever came back."

"Right. Well, on my coronation day, with Aslan's approval, I swore an oath that, if once I established peace in Narnia, I would sail east myself for a year and a day to find my father's friends or to learn of their deaths and avenge them if I could. These were their names: the Lord Revilian, the

Lord Bern, the Lord Argoz, the Lord Mavramorn, the Lord Octesian, the Lord Restimar, and—oh, that other one who's so hard to remember."

"The Lord Rhoop, Sire," said Drinian.

"Rhoop, Rhoop, of course," said Caspian. "That is my main intention. But Reepicheep here has an even higher hope." Everyone's eyes turned to the Mouse.

"As high as my spirit," it said. "Though perhaps as small as my stature. Why should we not come to the very eastern end of the world? And what might we find there? I expect to find Aslan's own country. It is always from the east, across the sea, that the great Lion comes to us."

"I say, that *is* an idea," said Edmund in an awed voice.

"But do you think," said Lucy, "Aslan's country would be that sort of country—I mean, the sort you could ever *sail* to?"

"I do not know, Madam," said Reepicheep. "But there is this. When I was in my cradle a wood woman, a Dryad, spoke this verse over me:

> "Where sky and water meet,
> Where the waves grow sweet,
> Doubt not, Reepicheep,
> To find all you seek,
> There is the utter East.

"I do not know what it means. But the spell of it has been on me all my life."

After a short silence Lucy asked, "And where are we now, Caspian?"

"The Captain can tell you better than I," said Caspian, so Drinian got out his chart and spread it on the table.

"That's our position," he said, laying his finger on it. "Or was at noon today. We had a fair wind from Cair Paravel and stood a little north for Galma, which we made on the next day. We were in port for a week, for the Duke of Galma made a great tournament for His Majesty and there he unhorsed many knights—"

"And got a few nasty falls myself, Drinian. Some of the bruises are there still," put in Caspian.

"—And unhorsed many knights," repeated Drinian with a grin. "We thought the Duke would have been pleased if the King's Majesty would have married his daughter, but nothing came of that—"

"Squints, and has freckles," said Caspian.

"Oh, poor girl," said Lucy.

"And we sailed from Galma," continued Drinian, "and ran into a calm for the best part of two days and had to row, and then had wind again and did not make Terebinthia till the fourth day from Galma. And there their King sent out a warning not to land for there was sickness in Terebinthia, but we doubled the cape and put in at a little creek far from the city and watered. Then we had to lie off for three days before we got a southeast wind and stood out for Seven Isles. The third day out a pirate (Terebinthian by her rig) overhauled us, but when she saw us well armed she stood off after some shooting of arrows on either part—"

"And we ought to have given her chase and boarded her and hanged every mother's son of them," said Reepicheep.

"—And in five days more we were in sight of Muil, which, as you know, is the westernmost of the Seven Isles. Then we rowed through the straits and came about sundown into Redhaven on the isle of Brenn, where we were very lovingly feasted and had victuals and water at will. We left Redhaven six days ago and have made marvelously good speed, so that I hope to see the Lone Islands the day after tomorrow. The sum is, we are now nearly thirty days at sea and have sailed more than four hundred leagues from Narnia."

"And after the Lone Islands?" said Lucy.

"No one knows, your Majesty," answered Drinian. "Unless the Lone Islanders themselves can tell us."

"They couldn't in our days," said Edmund.

"Then," said Reepicheep, "it is after the Lone Islands that the adventure really begins."

Caspian now suggested that they might like to

be shown over the ship before supper, but Lucy's conscience smote her and she said, "I think I really must go and see Eustace. Seasickness is horrid, you know. If I had my old cordial with me I could cure him."

"But you have," said Caspian. "I'd quite forgotten about it. As you left it behind I thought it might be regarded as one of the royal treasures and so I brought it—if you think it ought to be wasted on a thing like seasickness."

"It'll only take a drop," said Lucy.

Caspian opened one of the lockers beneath the bench and brought out the beautiful little diamond flask which Lucy remembered so well. "Take back your own, Queen," he said. They then left the cabin and went out into the sunshine.

In the deck there were two large, long hatches, fore and aft of the mast, and both open, as they always were in fair weather, to let light and air into the belly of the ship. Caspian led them down a ladder into the after hatch. Here they found themselves in a place where benches for rowing ran from side to side and the light came in through the oarholes and danced on the roof. Of course Caspian's ship was not that horrible thing, a galley rowed by slaves. Oars were used only when wind failed or for getting in and out of harbor and everyone (except Reepicheep whose legs were too short) had often taken a turn. At each side of the ship the space under the benches was left clear for the rowers' feet, but all down the center there was a kind of pit which went down to the very keel and this was filled with all kinds of things—sacks of flour, casks of water and beer, barrels of pork, jars of honey, skin bottles of wine, apples, nuts, cheeses, biscuits, turnips, sides of bacon. From the roof—that is, from the under side of the deck— hung hams and strings of onions, and also the men of the watch off-duty in their hammocks. Caspian led them aft, stepping from bench to bench; at least, it was stepping for him, and something be- tween a step and a jump for Lucy, and a real long jump for Reepicheep. In this way they came to a partition with a door in it. Caspian opened the door and led them into a cabin which filled the stern underneath the deck cabins in the poop. It was of course not so nice. It was very low and the sides sloped together as they went down so that there was hardly any floor; and though it had win- dows of thick glass, they were not made to open because they were under water. In fact at this very moment, as the ship pitched they were alternately golden with sunlight and dim green with the sea.

"You and I must lodge here, Edmund," said Caspian. "We'll leave your kinsman the bunk and sling hammocks for ourselves."

"I beseech your Majesty—" said Drinian.

"No, no shipmate," said Caspian, "we have argued all that out already. You and Rhince" (Rhince was the mate) "are sailing the ship and will have cares and labors many a night when we are singing catches or telling stories, so you and he must have the port cabin above. King Edmund and I can lie very snug here below. But how is the stranger?"

Eustace, very green in the face, scowled and asked whether there was any sign of the storm getting less. But Caspian said, "What storm?" and Drinian burst out laughing.

"Storm, young master!" he roared. "This is as

fair weather as a man could ask for."

"Who's that?" said Eustace irritably. "Send him away. His voice goes through my head."

"I've brought you something that will make you feel better, Eustace," said Lucy.

"Oh, go away and leave me alone," growled Eustace. But he took a drop from her flask, and though he said it was beastly stuff (the smell in the cabin when she opened it was delicious) it is certain that his face came the right color a few moments after he had swallowed it, and he must have felt better because, instead of wailing about the storm and his head, he began demanding to be put ashore and said that at the first port he would "lodge a disposition" against them all with the British Consul. But when Reepicheep asked what a disposition was and how you lodged it (Reepicheep thought it was some new way of arranging a single combat) Eustace could only reply, "Fancy not knowing that." In the end they succeeded in convincing Eustace that they were already sailing as fast as they could toward the nearest land they knew, and that they had no more power of sending him back to Cambridge—which was where Uncle Harold lived—than of sending him to the moon. After that he sulkily agreed to put on the fresh clothes which had been put out for him and come on deck.

Caspian now showed them over the ship,

though indeed they had seen most of it already. They went up on the forecastle and saw the look-out man standing on a little shelf inside the gilded dragon's neck and peering through its open mouth. Inside the forecastle was the galley (or ship's kitchen) and quarters for such people as the boatswain, the carpenter, the cook and the master-archer. If you think it odd to have the galley in the bows and imagine the smoke from its chimney streaming back over the ship, that is because you are thinking of steamships where there is always a headwind. On a sailing ship the wind is coming from behind, and anything smelly is put as far forward as possible. They were taken up to the fighting-top, and at first it was rather alarming to rock to and fro there and see the deck looking small and far away beneath. You realized that if you fell there was no particular reason why you should fall on board rather than in the sea. Then they were taken to the poop, where Rhince was on duty with another man at the great tiller, and behind that the dragon's tail rose up, covered with gilding, and round inside it ran a little bench. The name of the ship was *Dawn Treader*. She was only a little bit of a thing compared with one of our ships, or even with the cogs, dromonds, carracks and galleons which Narnia had owned when Lucy and Edmund had reigned there under Peter as the High King, for nearly all navigation had died out in the reigns of Caspian's ancestors. When his uncle, Miraz the usurper, had sent the seven lords to sea, they had had to buy a Galmian ship and man it with hired Galmian sailors. But now Caspian had begun to teach the Narnians to be sea-faring folk once more, and the *Dawn Treader* was the finest ship he had built yet. She was so small that, forward of the mast, there was hardly any deck room between the central hatch and the ship's boat on one side and the hen-coop (Lucy fed the hens) on the other. But she was a beauty of her kind, a "lady" as sailors say, her lines perfect, her colors pure, and every spar and rope and pin lovingly made. Eustace of course would be pleased with nothing, and kept on boasting about liners and motorboats and aeroplanes and submarines ("As if *he* knew anything about them," muttered Edmund), but the other two were delighted with the *Dawn Treader*, and when they returned aft to the cabin and supper, and saw the whole western sky lit up with an immense crimson sunset, and felt the quiver of the ship, and tasted the salt on their lips, and thought of unlands on the Eastern rim of the world, Lucy felt that she was almost too happy to speak.

What Eustace thought had best be told in his own words, for when they all got their clothes back, dried, next morning, he at once got out a little black notebook and a pencil and started to keep a diary. He always had this notebook with him and kept a record of his marks in it, for though he didn't care much about any subject for its own sake, he cared a great deal about marks and would even go to people and say, "I got so much. What did you get?" But as he didn't seem likely to get many marks on the *Dawn Treader* he now started a diary. This was the first entry.

"*August 7th.* Have now been twenty-four hours on this ghastly boat if it isn't a dream. All the time a frightful storm has been raging (it's a good thing I'm not seasick). Huge waves keep coming in over the front and I have seen the boat nearly go under any number of times. All the others pretend to take no notice of this, either from swank or because Harold says one of the most cowardly things ordinary people do is to shut their eyes to Facts. It's madness to come out into the sea in a rotten little thing like this. Not much bigger than a lifeboat. And, of course, absolutely primitive indoors. No proper saloon, no radio, no bathrooms, no deck-chairs. I was dragged all over it yesterday evening and it would make anyone sick to hear Caspian showing off his funny little toy boat as if it was the *Queen Mary*. I tried to tell him what real ships are like, but he's too dense. E. and L., *of course*, didn't back me up. I suppose a kid like L. doesn't realize the danger and E. is buttering up C. as everyone does here. They call him a King. I said I was a Republican but he had to ask me what that meant! He doesn't seem to know anything at all. *Needless to say* I've been put in the worst cabin of the boat, a perfect dungeon, and Lucy has been given a whole room on deck to herself, almost a nice room compared with the rest of this place. C. says that's because she's a girl. I tried to make him see what Alberta says, that all that sort of thing is really lowering girls but he was too dense. Still, he might see that I shall be ill if I'm kept in that *hole* any longer. E. says we mustn't grumble because C. is sharing it with us himself to make room for L. As if that didn't make it more crowded and far worse. Nearly forgot to say that there is also a kind of Mouse thing that gives everyone the most frightful cheek. The others can put up with it if they like but I shall twist his tail pretty soon if he tries it on me. The food is frightful too."

The trouble between Eustace and Reepicheep arrived even sooner than might have been expected. Before dinner next day, when the others were sitting round the table waiting (being at sea gives one a magnificent appetite), Eustace came rushing in, wringing his hand and shouting out:

"That little brute has half killed me. I insist on it being kept under control. I could bring an action against you, Caspian. I could order you to have it destroyed."

At the same moment Reepicheep appeared. His sword was drawn and his whiskers looked very fierce but he was as polite as ever.

"I ask your pardons all," he said, "and especially her Majesty's. If I had known that he would take refuge here I would have awaited a more reasonable time for his correction."

"What on earth's up?" asked Edmund.

What had really happened was this. Reepicheep, who never felt that the ship was getting on fast enough, loved to sit on the bulwarks far forward just beside the dragon's head, gazing out at the eastern horizon and singing softly in his little chirruping voice the song the Dryad had made for him. He never held on to anything, however the ship pitched, and kept his balance with perfect ease; perhaps his long tail, hanging down to the deck inside the bulwarks, made this easier. Everyone on board was familiar with this habit, and the sailors liked it because when one was on look-out duty it gave one somebody to talk to. Why exactly Eustace had slipped and reeled and stumbled all the way forward to the forecastle (he had not yet got his sea-legs) I never heard. Perhaps he hoped he would see land, or perhaps he wanted to hang about the galley and scrounge something. Anyway, as soon as he saw that long tail hanging down—and perhaps it was rather tempting—he thought it would be delightful to catch hold of it, swing Reepicheep round by it once or twice upside-down, then run away and laugh. At first the plan seemed to work beautifully. The Mouse was not much heavier than a very large cat. Eustace had him off the rail in a trice and very silly he looked (thought Eustace) with his little limbs all splayed out and his mouth open. But unfortunately Reepicheep, who had fought for his life many a time, never lost his head even for a moment. Nor his skill. It is not very easy to draw one's sword when one is swinging round in the air by one's tail, but he did. And the next thing Eustace knew was two agonizing jabs in his hand which made him let go of the tail; and the next thing after that was that the Mouse had picked itself up again as if it were a ball bouncing off the deck, and there it was facing him, and a horrid long, bright, sharp thing like a skewer was waving to and fro within an inch of his stomach. (This doesn't count as below the belt for mice in Narnia because they can hardly be expected to reach higher.)

"Stop it," spluttered Eustace, "go away. Put that thing away. It's not safe. Stop it, I say. I'll tell Caspian. I'll have you muzzled and tied up."

"Why do you not draw your own sword, poltroon!" cheeped the Mouse. "Draw and fight or I'll beat you black and blue with the flat."

"I haven't got one," said Eustace. "I'm a pacifist. I don't believe in fighting."

"Do I understand," said Reepicheep, withdrawing his sword for a moment and speaking very sternly, "that you do not intend to give me satisfaction?"

"I don't know what you mean," said Eustace, nursing his hand. "If you don't know how to take a joke I shan't bother my head about you."

"Then take that," said Reepicheep, "and that— to teach you manners—and the respect due to a knight—and a Mouse—and a Mouse's tail—" and at each word he gave Eustace a blow with the side of his rapier, which was thin, fine, dwarf-tempered steel and as supple and effective as a birch rod. Eustace (of course) was at a school where they didn't have corporal punishment, so the sensation was quite new to him. That was why, in spite of having no sea-legs, it took him less than a minute to get off that forecastle and cover the whole length of the deck and burst in at the cabin door— still hotly pursued by Reepicheep. Indeed it seemed to Eustace that the rapier as well as the pursuit was hot. It might have been red-hot by the feel.

There was not much difficulty in settling the matter once Eustace realized that everyone took the idea of a duel seriously and heard Caspian offering to lend him a sword, and Drinian and Edmund discussing whether he ought to be handicapped in some way to make up for his being so much bigger than Reepicheep. He apologized sulkily and went off with Lucy to have his hand bathed and bandaged and then went to his bunk. He was careful to lie on his side.

THE LONE ISLANDS

"LAND IN SIGHT," SHOUTED THE MAN IN the bows.

Lucy, who had been talking to Rhince on the poop, came pattering down the ladder and raced forward. As she went she was joined by Edmund, and they found Caspian, Drinian and Reepicheep already on the forecastle. It was a coldish morning, the sky very pale and the sea very dark blue with little white caps of foam, and there, a little way off on the starboard bow, was the nearest of the Lone Islands, Felimath, like a low green hill in the sea, and behind it, further off, the gray slopes of its sister Doorn.

"Same old Felimath! Same old Doorn," said Lucy, clapping her hands. "Oh—Edmund, how long it is since you and I saw them last!"

"I've never understood why they belong to Narnia," said Caspian. "Did Peter the High King conquer them?"

"Oh no," said Edmund. "They were Narnian

before our time—in the days of the White Witch."

(By the way, I have never yet heard how these remote islands became attached to the crown of Narnia; if I ever do, and if the story is at all interesting, I may put it in some other book.)

"Are we to put in here, Sire?" asked Drinian.

"I shouldn't think it would be much good landing on Felimath," said Edmund. "It was almost uninhabited in our days and it looks as if it was the same still. The people lived mostly on Doorn and a little on Avra—that's the third one; you can't see it yet. They only kept sheep on Felimath."

"Then we'll have to double that cape, I suppose," said Drinian, "and land on Doorn. That'll mean rowing."

"I'm sorry we're not landing on Felimath," said Lucy. "I'd like to walk there again. It was so lonely—a nice kind of loneliness, and all grass and clover and soft sea air."

"I'd love to stretch my legs too," said Caspian. "I tell you what. Why shouldn't we go ashore in the boat and send it back, and then we could walk across Felimath and let the *Dawn Treader* pick us up on the other side?"

If Caspian had been as experienced then as he became later on in this voyage he would not have made this suggestion; but at the moment it seemed an excellent one. "Oh do let's," said Lucy.

"You'll come, will you?" said Caspian to Eustace,

who had come on deck with his hand bandaged.

"Anything to get off this blasted boat," said Eustace.

"Blasted?" said Drinian. "How do you mean?"

"In a civilized country like where I come from," said Eustace, "the ships are so big that when you're inside you wouldn't know you were at sea at all."

"In that case you might just as well stay ashore," said Caspian. "Will you tell them to lower the boat, Drinian?"

The King, the Mouse, the two Pevensies, and Eustace all got into the boat and were pulled to the beach of Felimath. When the boat had left them and was being rowed back they all turned and looked round. They were surprised at how small the *Dawn Treader* looked.

Lucy was of course barefoot, having kicked off her shoes while swimming, but that is no hardship if one is going to walk on downy turf. It was delightful to be ashore again and to smell the earth and grass, even if at first the ground seemed to be pitching up and down like a ship, as it usually does for a while if one has been at sea. It was much warmer here than it had been on board and Lucy found the sand pleasant to her feet as they crossed it. There was a lark singing.

They struck inland and up a fairly steep, though low, hill. At the top of course they looked back, and there was the *Dawn Treader* shining like a great bright insect and crawling slowly north-westward with her oars. Then they went over the ridge and could see her no longer.

Doorn now lay before them, divided from Felimath by a channel about a mile wide; behind it and to the left lay Avra. The little white town of Narrowhaven on Doorn was easily seen.

"Hullo! What's this?" said Edmund suddenly.

In the green valley to which they were descending six or seven rough-looking men, all armed, were sitting by a tree.

"Don't tell them who we are," said Caspian.

"And pray, your Majesty, why not?" said Reepicheep who had consented to ride on Lucy's shoulder.

"It just occurred to me," replied Caspian, "that no one here can have heard from Narnia for a long time. It's just possible they may not still acknowledge our over-lordship. In which case it might not be quite safe to be known as the King."

"We have our swords, Sire," said Reepicheep.

"Yes, Reep, I know we have," said Caspian. "But if it is a question of re-conquering the three islands, I'd prefer to come back with a rather larger army."

By this time they were quite close to the strangers, one of whom—a big black-haired fellow—shouted out, "A good morning to you."

"And a good morning to you," said Caspian. "Is there still a Governor of the Lone Islands?"

"To be sure there is," said the man, "Governor Gumpas. His Sufficiency is at Narrowhaven. But you'll stay and drink with us."

Caspian thanked him, though neither he nor the

others much liked the look of their new acquaintance, and all of them sat down. But hardly had they raised their cups to their lips when the black-haired man nodded to his companions and, as quick as lightning, all the five visitors found themselves wrapped in strong arms. There was a moment's struggle but all the advantages were on one side, and soon everyone was disarmed and had their hands tied behind their backs—except Reepicheep, writhing in his captor's grip and biting furiously.

"Careful with that beast, Tacks," said the Leader. "Don't damage him. He'll fetch the best price of the lot, I shouldn't wonder."

"Coward! Poltroon!" squeaked Reepicheep. "Give me my sword and free my paws if you dare."

"Whew!" whistled the slave merchant (for that is what he was). "It can talk! Well I never did. Blowed if I take less than two hundred crescents for him." The Calormen crescent, which is the chief coin in those parts, is worth about a third of a pound.

"So that's what you are," said Caspian. "A kidnapper and slaver. I hope you're proud of it."

"Now, now, now, now," said the slaver. "Don't you start any jaw. The easier you take it, the pleasanter all round, see? I don't do this for fun. I've got my living to make same as anyone else."

"Where will you take us?" asked Lucy, getting the words out with some difficulty.

"Over to Narrowhaven," said the slaver. "For market day tomorrow."

"Is there a British Consul there?" asked Eustace.

"Is there a which?" said the man.

But long before Eustace was tired of trying to explain, the slaver simply said, "Well, I've had enough of this jabber. The Mouse is a fair treat but this one would talk the hind leg off a donkey. Off we go, mates."

Then the four human prisoners were roped together, not cruelly but securely, and made to march down to the shore. Reepicheep was carried. He had stopped biting on a threat of having his mouth tied up, but he had a great deal to say, and

Lucy really wondered how any man could bear to have the things said to him which were said to the slave dealer by the Mouse. But the slave dealer, far from objecting, only said "Go on" whenever Reepicheep paused for breath, occasionally adding, "It's as good as a play," or, "Blimey, you can't help almost thinking it knows what it's saying!" or "Was it one of you what trained it?" This so infuriated Reepicheep that in the end the number of things he thought of saying all at once nearly suffocated him and he became silent.

When they got down to the shore that looked toward Doorn they found a little village and a long-boat on the beach and, lying a little further out, a dirty bedraggled looking ship.

"Now, youngsters," said the slave dealer, "let's have no fuss and then you'll have nothing to cry about. All aboard."

At that moment a fine-looking bearded man came out of one of the houses (an inn, I think) and said:

"Well, Pug. More of your usual wares?"

The slaver, whose name seemed to be Pug, bowed very low, and said in a wheedling kind of voice, "Yes, please your Lordship."

"How much do you want for that boy?" asked the other, pointing to Caspian.

"Ah," said Pug, "I knew your Lordship would pick on the best. No deceiving your Lordship with anything second rate. That boy, now, I've taken a fancy to him myself. Got kind of fond of him, I have. I'm that tender-hearted I didn't ever ought to have taken up this job. Still, to a customer like your Lordship—"

"Tell me your price, carrion," said the Lord sternly. "Do you think I want to listen to the rigmarole of your filthy trade?"

"Three hundred crescents, my Lord, to your honorable Lordship, but to anyone else—"

"I'll give you a hundred and fifty."

"Oh please, please," broke in Lucy. "Don't separate us, whatever you do. You don't know—" But then she stopped for she saw that Caspian didn't even now want to be known.

"A hundred and fifty, then," said the Lord. "As for you, little maiden, I am sorry I cannot buy you all. Unrope my boy, Pug. And look—treat these others well while they are in your hands or it'll be the worse for you."

"Well!" said Pug. "Now who ever heard of a gentleman in my way of business who treated his stock better than what I do? Well? Why, I treat 'em like my own children."

"That's likely enough to be true," said the other grimly.

The dreadful moment had now come. Caspian was untied and his new master said, "This way, lad," and Lucy burst into tears and Edmund looked very blank. But Caspian looked over his shoulder and said, "Cheer up. I'm sure it will come all right in the end. So long."

"Now, missie," said Pug. "Don't you start taking on and spoiling your looks for the market tomorrow. You be a good girl and then you won't have nothing to cry *about*, see?"

Then they were rowed out to the slave-ship and taken below into a long, rather dark place, none too clean, where they found many other unfortunate prisoners; for Pug was of course a pirate and had just returned from cruising among the islands and capturing what he could. The children didn't meet anyone whom they knew; the prisoners were mostly Galmians and Terebinthians. And there they sat in the straw and wondered what was happening to Caspian and tried to stop Eustace talking as if everyone except himself was to blame.

Meanwhile Caspian was having a much more interesting time. The man who had bought him led him down a little lane between two of the village houses and so out into an open place behind the village. Then he turned and faced him.

"You needn't be afraid of me, boy," he said. "I'll treat you well. I bought you for your face. You reminded me of someone."

"May I ask of whom, my Lord?" said Caspian.

"You remind me of my master, King Caspian of Narnia."

Then Caspian decided to risk everything on one stroke.

"My Lord," he said, "I *am* your master. I am Caspian, King of Narnia."

"You make very free," said the other. "How shall I know this is true?"

"Firstly by my face," said Caspian. "Secondly because I know within six guesses who you are. You are one of those seven lords of Narnia whom my Uncle Miraz sent to sea and whom I have come out to look for—Argoz, Bern, Octesian, Restimar, Mavramorn, or—or—I have forgotten the others. And finally, if your Lordship will give me a sword I will prove on any man's body in clean battle that I am Caspian the son of Caspian, lawful King of Narnia, Lord of Cair Paravel, and Emperor of the Lone Islands."

"By heaven," exclaimed the man, "it is his father's very voice and trick of speech. My liege—your Majesty—" And there in the field he knelt and kissed the King's hand.

"The moneys your Lordship disbursed for our person will be made good from our own treasury," said Caspian.

"They're not in Pug's purse yet, Sire," said the Lord Bern, for he it was. "And never will be, I trust. I have moved His Sufficiency the Governor a hundred times to crush this vile traffic in man's flesh."

"My Lord Bern," said Caspian, "we must talk of the state of these Islands. But first what is your Lordship's own story?"

"Short enough, Sire," said Bern. "I came thus far with my six fellows, loved a girl of the islands, and felt I had had enough of the sea. And there was no purpose in returning to Narnia while your Majesty's uncle held the reins. So I married and have lived here ever since."

"And what is this governor, this Gumpas, like? Does he still acknowledge the King of Narnia for his lord?"

"In words, yes. All is done in the King's name. But he would not be best pleased to find a real, live King of Narnia coming in upon him. And if your Majesty came before him alone and unarmed—well he would not deny his allegiance, but he would pretend to disbelieve you. Your Grace's life would be in danger. What following has your

Majesty in these waters?"

"There is my ship just rounding the point," said Caspian. "We are about thirty swords if it came to fighting. Shall we not have my ship in and fall upon Pug and free my friends whom he holds captive?"

"Not by my counsel," said Bern. "As soon as there was a fight two or three ships would put out from Narrowhaven to rescue Pug. Your Majesty must work by a show of more power than you really have, and by the terror of the King's name. It must not come to plain battle. Gumpas is a chicken-hearted man and can be over-awed."

After a little more conversation Caspian and Bern walked down to the coast a little west of the village and there Caspian winded his horn. (This was not the great magic horn of Narnia, Queen Susan's Horn: he had left that at home for his regent Trumpkin to use if any great need fell upon the land in the King's absence.) Drinian, who was on the lookout for a signal, recognized the royal horn at once and the *Dawn Treader* began standing in to shore. Then the boat put off again and in a few moments Caspian and the Lord Bern were on deck explaining the situation to Drinian. He, just like Caspian, wanted to lay the *Dawn Treader* alongside the slave-ship at once and board her, but Bern made the same objection.

"Steer straight down this channel, captain," said Bern, "and then round to Avra where my own

estates are. But first run up the King's banner,
hang out all the shields, and send as many men to
the fighting-top as you can. And about five bow-
shots hence, when you get open sea on your port
bow, run up a few signals."

"Signals? To whom?" said Drinian.

"Why, to all the other ships we haven't got but
which it might be well that Gumpas thinks we
have."

"Oh, I see," said Drinian, rubbing his hands.
"And they'll read our signals. What shall I say?
*Whole fleet round the South of Avra and assemble
at—?*"

"Bernstead," said the Lord Bern. "That'll do ex-
cellently. Their whole journey—if there *were* any
ships—would be out of sight from Narrowhaven."

Caspian was sorry for the others languishing in
the hold of Pug's slave-ship, but he could not help
finding the rest of that day enjoyable. Late in the
afternoon (for they had to do all by oar), having
turned to starboard round the northeast end of
Doorn and port again round the point of Avra,
they entered into a good harbor on Avra's southern shore where Bern's pleasant lands sloped down
to the water's edge. Bern's people, many of whom
they saw working in the fields, were all freemen
and it was a happy and prosperous fief. Here they
all went ashore and were royally feasted in a low,
pillared house overlooking the bay. Bern and his

gracious wife and merry daughters made them good cheer. But after dark Bern sent a messenger over by boat to Doorn to order some preparations (he did not say exactly what) for the following day.

WHAT CASPIAN
DID THERE

NEXT MORNING THE LORD BERN CALLED his guests early, and after breakfast he asked Caspian to order every man he had into full armor. "And above all," he added, "let everything be as trim and scoured as if it were the morning of the first battle in a great war between noble kings with all the world looking on." This was done; and then in three boatloads Caspian and his people, and Bern with a few of his, put out for Narrowhaven. The King's flag flew in the stern of his boat and his trumpeter was with him.

When they reached the jetty at Narrowhaven, Caspian found a considerable crowd assembled to meet them. "This is what I sent word about last night," said Bern. "They are all friends of mine and honest people." And as soon as Caspian stepped ashore the crowd broke out into hurrahs and shouts of, "Narnia! Narnia! Long live the King." At the same moment—and this was also due to Bern's messengers—bells began ringing from many parts of the town. Then Caspian caused his banner to be advanced and his trumpet to be blown and every man drew his sword and set his face into a joyful sternness, and they marched up the street so that the street shook, and their armor shone (for it was a sunny morning) so that one could hardly look at it steadily.

At first the only people who cheered were those who had been warned by Bern's messenger and knew what was happening and wanted it to happen. But then all the children joined in because they liked a procession and had seen very few. And then all the schoolboys joined in because they also liked processions and felt that the more noise and disturbance there was the less likely they would be to have any school that morning. And then all the old women put their heads out of doors and windows and began chattering and cheering because it was a king, and what is a governor compared with that? And all the young women joined in for the same reason and also because Caspian and Drinian and the rest were so handsome. And then all the young men came to see what the young women were looking at, so that by the time Caspian reached the castle gates, nearly the whole town was shouting; and where Gumpas sat in the castle, muddling and messing about with accounts and forms and rules and regulations, he heard the noise.

At the castle gate Caspian's trumpeter blew a blast and cried, "Open for the King of Narnia, come to visit his trusty and well-beloved servant the governor of the Lone Islands." In those days everything in the islands was done in a slovenly, slouching manner. Only the little postern opened, and out came a tousled fellow with a dirty old hat on his head instead of a helmet, and a rusty old pike in his hand. He blinked at the flashing figures before him. "Carn—seez—fishansy," he mumbled (which was his way of saying, "You can't see His Sufficiency"). "No interviews without 'pointments 'cept 'tween nine 'n' ten p.m. second Saturday every month."

"Uncover before Narnia, you dog," thundered the Lord Bern, and dealt him a rap with his gauntleted hand which sent his hat flying from his head.

"'Ere? Wot's it all about?" began the door-keeper, but no one took any notice of him. Two of Caspian's men stepped through the postern and after some struggling with bars and bolts (for everything was rusty) flung both wings of the gate wide open. Then the King and his followers strode into the courtyard. Here a number of the governor's guards were lounging about and several more (they were mostly wiping their mouths) came tumbling out of various doorways. Though their armor was in a disgraceful condition, these were fellows who might have fought if they had been led or had known what was happening; so this was the dangerous moment. Caspian gave them no time to think.

"Where is the captain?" he asked.

"I am, more or less, if you know what I mean," said a languid and rather dandified young person without any armor at all.

"It is our wish," said Caspian, "that our royal visitation to our realm of the Lone Islands should, if possible, be an occasion of joy and not of terror to our loyal subjects. If it were not for that, I should have something to say about the state of your men's armor and weapons. As it is, you are pardoned. Command a cask of wine to be opened that your men may drink our health. But at noon tomorrow I wish to see them here in this courtyard looking like men-at-arms and not like vagabonds. See to it on pain of our extreme displeasure."

The captain gaped but Bern immediately cried, "Three cheers for the King," and the soldiers, who had understood about the cask of wine even if they understood nothing else, joined in. Caspian then ordered most of his own men to remain in the courtyard. He, with Bern and Drinian and four others, went into the hall.

Behind a table at the far end with various secretaries about him sat his Sufficiency, the Governor of the Lone Islands. Gumpas was a bilious-looking man with hair that had once been red and was now mostly gray. He glanced up as the strangers entered and then looked down at his papers saying automatically, "No interviews without appointments except between nine and ten p.m. on second Saturdays."

Caspian nodded to Bern and then stood aside. Bern and Drinian took a step forward and each seized one end of the table. They lifted it, and flung it on one side of the hall where it rolled over, scattering a cascade of letters, dossiers, inkpots, pens, sealing-wax and documents. Then, not roughly but as firmly as if their hands were pincers of steel, they plucked Gumpas out of his chair and deposited him, facing it, about four feet away.

Caspian at once sat down in the chair and laid his naked sword across his knees.

"My Lord," said he, fixing his eyes on Gumpas, "you have not given us quite the welcome we expected. We are the King of Narnia."

"Nothing about it in the correspondence," said the governor. "Nothing in the minutes. We have not been notified of any such thing. All irregular. Happy to consider any applications—"

"And we are come to inquire into your Sufficiency's conduct of your office," continued Caspian. "There are two points especially on which I require an explanation. Firstly I find no record that the tribute due from these Islands to the crown of Narnia has been received for about a hundred and fifty years."

"That would be a question to raise at the Council next month," said Gumpas. "If anyone moves that a commission of inquiry be set up to report on the financial history of the islands at the first meeting next year, why then . . ."

"I also find it very clearly written in our laws," Caspian went on, "that if the tribute is not delivered the whole debt has to be paid by the Governor of the Lone Islands out of his private purse."

At this Gumpas began to pay real attention. "Oh, that's quite out of the question," he said. "It is an economic impossibility—er—your Majesty must be joking."

Inside, he was wondering if there were any way of getting rid of these unwelcome visitors. Had he known that Caspian had only one ship and one ship's company with him, he would have spoken soft words for the moment, and hoped to have them all surrounded and killed during the night. But he had seen a ship of war sail down the straits yesterday and seen it signaling, as he supposed, to its consorts. He had not then known it was the King's ship for there was not wind enough to spread the flag out and make the golden lion visible, so he had waited further developments. Now he imagined that Caspian had a whole fleet at Bernstead. It would never have occurred to Gumpas that anyone would walk into Narrowhaven to take the islands with less than fifty men; it was certainly not at all the kind of thing he could imagine doing himself.

"Secondly," said Caspian, "I want to know why you have permitted this abominable and unnatural traffic in slaves to grow up here, contrary to the ancient custom and usage of our dominions."

"Necessary, unavoidable," said his Sufficiency. "An essential part of the economic development of the islands, I assure you. Our present burst of prosperity depends on it."

"What need have you of slaves?"

"For export, your Majesty. Sell 'em to Calormen mostly; and we have other markets. We are a great center of the trade."

"In other words," said Caspian, "you don't need them. Tell me what purpose they serve except to put money into the pockets of such as Pug?"

"Your Majesty's tender years," said Gumpas, with what was meant to be a fatherly smile, "hardly make it possible that you should understand the economic problem involved. I have statistics, I have graphs, I have—"

"Tender as my years may be," said Caspian, "I believe I understand the slave trade from within quite as well as your Sufficiency. And I do not see that it brings into the islands meat or bread or beer or wine or timber or cabbages or books or instruments of music or horses or armor or anything else worth having. But whether it does or not, it must be stopped."

"But that would be putting the clock back," gasped the governor. "Have you no idea of progress, of development?"

"I have seen them both in an egg," said Caspian. "We call it 'Going Bad' in Narnia. This trade must stop."

"I can take no responsibility for any such measure," said Gumpas.

"Very well, then," answered Caspian, "we relieve you of your office. My Lord Bern, come here." And before Gumpas quite realized what was happening, Bern was kneeling with his hands between the King's hands and taking the oath to govern the Lone Islands in accordance with the old customs, rights, usages and laws of Narnia. And Caspian said, "I think we have had enough of governors," and made Bern a Duke, the Duke of the Lone Islands.

"As for you, my Lord," he said to Gumpas, "I forgive you your debt for the tribute. But before noon tomorrow you and yours must be out of the castle, which is now the Duke's residence."

"Look here, this is all very well," said one of Gumpas's secretaries, "but suppose all you gentlemen stop play-acting and we do a little business. The question before us really is—"

"The question is," said the Duke, "whether you and the rest of the rabble will leave without a flogging or with one. You may choose which you prefer."

When all this had been pleasantly settled, Caspian ordered horses, of which there were a few in the castle, though very ill-groomed, and he, with Bern and Drinian and a few others, rode out into the town and made for the slave market. It was a long low building near the harbor and the scene which they found going on inside was very much like any other auction; that is to say, there was a great crowd and Pug, on a platform, was roaring out in a raucous voice:

"Now, gentlemen, lot twenty-three. Fine Terebinthian agricultural laborer, suitable for the mines or the galleys. Under twenty-five years of age. Not a bad tooth in his head. Good, brawny fellow. Take off his shirt, Tacks, and let the gentlemen see. There's muscle for you! Look at the chest on him. Ten crescents from the gentleman in the corner. You must be joking, sir. Fifteen! Eighteen! Eighteen is bidden for lot twenty-three. Any advance on eighteen? Twenty-one. Thank you, sir. Twenty-one is bidden—"

But Pug stopped and gaped when he saw the mail-clad figures who had clanked up to the platform.

"On your knees, every man of you, to the King of Narnia," said the Duke. Everyone heard the horses jingling and stamping outside and many had heard some rumor of the landing and the events at the castle. Most obeyed. Those who did not were pulled down by their neighbors. Some cheered.

"Your life is forfeit, Pug, for laying hands on our royal person yesterday," said Caspian. "But your ignorance is pardoned. The slave trade was forbidden in all our dominions quarter of an hour ago. I declare every slave in this market free."

He held up his hand to check the cheering of the slaves and went on, "Where are my friends?"

"That dear little gel and the nice young gentleman?" said Pug with an ingratiating smile. "Why, they were snapped up at once—"

"We're here, we're here, Caspian," cried Lucy and Edmund together and, "At your service, Sire," piped Reepicheep from another corner. They had all been sold but the men who had bought them were staying to bid for other slaves and so they had not yet been taken away. The crowd parted to let the three of them out and there was great hand-clasping and greeting between them and Caspian. Two merchants of Calormen at once approached. The Calormen have dark faces and long beards. They wear flowing robes and orange-colored turbans, and they are a wise, wealthy, courteous, cruel and ancient people. They bowed most politely to Caspian and paid him long compliments, all about the fountains of prosperity irrigating the gardens of prudence and virtue—and things like that—but of course what they wanted was the money they had paid.

"That is only fair, sirs," said Caspian. "Every man who has bought a slave today must have his money back. Pug, bring out your takings to the last minim." (A minim is the fortieth part of a crescent.)

"Does your good Majesty mean to beggar me?" whined Pug.

"You have lived on broken hearts all your life," said Caspian, "and if you *are* beggared, it is better to be a beggar than a slave. But where is my other friend?"

"Oh *him?*" said Pug. "Oh take *him* and welcome. Glad to have him off my hands. I've never seen such a drug in the market in all my born days. Priced him at five crescents in the end and even so nobody'd have him. Threw him in free with other lots and still no one would have him. Wouldn't touch him. Wouldn't look at him. Tacks, bring out Sulky."

Thus Eustace was produced, and sulky he certainly looked; for though no one would want to be sold as a slave, it is perhaps even more galling to be a sort of utility slave whom no one will buy. He walked up to Caspian and said, "I see. As usual. Been enjoying yourself somewhere while the rest of us were prisoners. I suppose you haven't even found out about the British Consul. Of course not."

That night they had a great feast in the castle of Narrowhaven and then, "Tomorrow for the beginning of our real adventures!" said Reepicheep when he had made his bows to everyone and went to bed. But it could not really be tomorrow or anything like it. For now they were preparing to leave all known lands and seas behind them and the fullest preparations had to be made. The *Dawn Treader* was emptied and drawn on land by eight horses over rollers and every bit of her was gone over by the most skilled shipwrights. Then she was launched again and victualed and watered as full as she could hold—that is to say for twenty-eight days. Even this, as Edmund noticed with disappointment, only gave them a fortnight's eastward sailing before they had to abandon their quest.

While all this was being done Caspian missed no chance of questioning all the oldest sea captains whom he could find in Narrowhaven to learn if they had any knowledge or even any rumors of

land further to the east. He poured out many a flagon of the castle ale to weather-beaten men with short gray beards and clear blue eyes, and many a tall yarn he heard in return. But those who seemed the most truthful could tell of no lands beyond the Lone Islands, and many thought that if you sailed too far east you would come into the surges of a sea without lands that swirled perpetually round the rim of the world—"And that, I reckon, is where your Majesty's friends went to the bottom." The rest had only wild stories of islands inhabited by headless men, floating islands, waterspouts, and a fire that burned along the water. Only one, to Reepicheep's delight, said, "And beyond that, Aslan's country. But that's beyond the end of the world and you can't get there." But when they questioned him he could only say that he'd heard it from his father.

Bern could only tell them that he had seen his six companions sail away eastward and that nothing had ever been heard of them again. He said this when he and Caspian were standing on the highest point of Avra looking down on the eastern ocean. "I've often been up here of a morning," said the Duke, "and seen the sun come up out of the sea, and sometimes it looked as if it were only a couple of miles away. And I've wondered about my friends and wondered what there really is behind that horizon. Nothing, most likely, yet I am always half ashamed that I stayed behind. But I wish your Majesty wouldn't go. We may need your help here. This closing the slave market might make a new world; war with Calormen is what I foresee. My liege, think again."

"I have an oath, my lord Duke," said Caspian. "And anyway, what *could* I say to Reepicheep?"

Five

THE STORM
AND WHAT CAME OF IT

IT WAS NEARLY THREE WEEKS AFTER their landing that the *Dawn Treader* was towed out of Narrowhaven harbor. Very solemn farewells had been spoken and a great crowd had assembled to see her departure. There had been cheers, and tears too, when Caspian made his last speech to the Lone Islanders and parted from the Duke and his family, but as the ship, her purple sail still flapping idly, drew further from the shore, and the sound of Caspian's trumpet from the poop came fainter across the water, everyone became silent. Then she came into the wind. The sail swelled out, the tug cast off and began rowing back, the first real wave ran up under the *Dawn Treader*'s prow, and she was a live ship again. The men off duty went below, Drinian took the first watch on the poop, and she turned her head eastward round the south of Avra.

The next few days were delightful. Lucy

thought she was the most fortunate girl in the world, as she woke each morning to see the reflections of the sunlit water dancing on the ceiling of her cabin and looked round on all the nice new things she had got in the Lone Islands—seaboots and buskins and cloaks and jerkins and scarves. And then she would go on deck and take a look from the forecastle at a sea which was a brighter blue each morning and drink in an air that was a little warmer day by day. After that came breakfast and such an appetite as one only has at sea.

She spent a good deal of time sitting on the little bench in the stern playing chess with Reepicheep. It was amusing to see him lifting the pieces, which were far too big for him, with both paws and standing on tiptoes if he made a move near the center of the board. He was a good player and when he remembered what he was doing usually won. But every now and then Lucy won because the Mouse did something quite ridiculous like sending a knight into the danger of a queen and castle combined. This happened because he had momentarily forgotten it was a game of chess and was thinking of a real battle and making the knight do what he would certainly have done in its place. For his mind was full of forlorn hopes, death-or-glory charges, and last stands.

But this pleasant time did not last. There came an evening when Lucy, gazing idly astern at the long furrow or wake they were leaving behind them, saw a great rack of clouds building itself up in the west with amazing speed. Then a gap was torn in it and a yellow sunset poured through the gap. All the waves behind them seemed to take on unusual shapes and the sea was a drab or yellowish color like dirty canvas. The air grew cold. The ship seemed to move uneasily as if she felt danger behind her. The sail would be flat and limp one minute and wildly full the next. While she was noting these things and wondering at a sinister change which had come over the very noise of the wind, Drinian cried, "All hands on deck." In a moment everyone became frantically busy. The hatches were battened down, the galley fire was put out, men went aloft to reef the sail. Before they had finished the storm struck them. It seemed to Lucy that a great valley in the sea opened just before their bows, and they rushed down into it, deeper down than she would have believed possible. A great gray hill of water, far higher than the mast, rushed to meet them; it looked certain death but they were tossed to the top of it. Then the ship seemed to spin round. A cataract of water poured over the deck; the poop and forecastle were like two islands with a fierce sea between them. Up aloft the sailors were lying out along the yard desperately trying to get control of the sail. A broken rope stood out sideways in the wind as straight and stiff as if it was a poker.

"Get below, Ma'am," bawled Drinian. And Lucy, knowing that landsmen—and landswomen—are a nuisance to the crew, began to obey. It was not easy. The *Dawn Treader* was listing terribly to starboard and the deck sloped like the roof of a house. She had to clamber round to the top of the ladder, holding on to the rail, and then stand by while two men climbed up it, and then get down it as best she could. It was well she was already holding on tight for at the foot of the ladder another wave roared across the deck, up to her shoulders. She was already almost wet through with spray and rain but this was colder. Then she made a dash for the cabin door and got in and shut out for a moment the appalling sight of the speed with which they were rushing into the dark, but not of course the horrible confusion of creakings, groanings, snappings, clatterings, roarings and boomings which only sounded more alarming below than they had done on the poop.

And all next day and all the next it went on. It went on till one could hardly even remember a time before it had begun. And there always had to be three men at the tiller and it was as much as three could do to keep any kind of a course. And there always had to be men at the pump. And there was hardly any rest for anyone, and nothing could be cooked and nothing could be dried, and one man was lost overboard, and they never saw the sun.

When it was over Eustace made the following entry in his diary:

"*September 3.* The first day for ages when I have been able to write. We had been driven before a hurricane for thirteen days and nights. I know that because I kept a careful count, though the others all say it was only twelve. *Pleasant* to be embarked on a dangerous voyage with people who can't even count right! I have had a ghastly time, up and down enormous waves hour after hour, usually wet to the skin, and not even an *attempt* at giving us proper meals. Needless to say there's no wireless or even a rocket, so no chance of signaling anyone for help. It all proves what I keep on telling them, the madness of setting out in a rotten little tub like this. It would be bad enough even if one was with decent people instead of fiends in human form. Caspian and Edmund are simply brutal to me. The night we lost our mast (there's only a stump left now), though I was *not at all* well, they forced me to come on deck and work like a slave. Lucy shoved her oar in by saying that Reepicheep was longing to go only he was too small. I wonder she doesn't see that everything that little beast does is all for the sake of *showing off.* Even at her age she ought to have that amount of sense. Today the beastly boat is level at last and the sun's out and we have all been jawing about what to do. We have food enough, pretty beastly stuff most of it, to last for sixteen days. (The poultry were all washed overboard. Even if they hadn't been, the storm would have stopped them laying.) The real trouble is water. Two casks seem to have got a leak knocked in them and are empty. (Narnian efficiency again.) On short rations, half a pint a day each, we've got enough for twelve days. (There's still lots of rum and wine but even *they* realize that would only make them thirstier.)

"If we could, of course, the sensible thing would be to turn west at once and make for the Lone Islands. But it took us eighteen days to get where we are, running like mad with a gale behind us. Even if we got an east wind it might take us far longer to get back. And at present there's no sign of an east wind—in fact there's no wind at all. As for rowing back, it would take far too long and Caspian says the men couldn't row on half a pint of water a day. I'm pretty sure this is wrong. I tried to explain that perspiration really cools people down, so the men would need less water if they were working. He didn't take any notice of this, which is always his way when he can't think of an answer. The others all voted for going *on* in the hope of finding land. I felt it my duty to point out that we didn't know there *was* any land ahead and tried to get them to see the dangers of *wishful thinking.* Instead of producing a better plan they had the cheek to ask me what I proposed. So I just explained coolly and quietly that I had been kidnapped and brought away on this *idiotic* voyage without my consent, and it was hardly *my* business to get *them* out of their scrape.

"*September 4.* Still becalmed. Very short rations for dinner and I got less than anyone. Caspian is very clever at helping and thinks I don't see! Lucy for some reason tried to make up to me by offering me some of hers but that *interfering prig* Edmund wouldn't let her. Pretty hot sun. Terribly thirsty all evening.

"*September 5.* Still becalmed and very hot.

Feeling rotten all day and am sure I've got a temperature. Of course they haven't the sense to keep a thermometer on board.

"*September 6.* A horrible day. Woke up in the night *knowing* I was feverish and *must* have a drink of water. Any doctor would have said so. Heaven knows I'm the last person to try to get any unfair advantage but I never *dreamed* that this water-rationing would be meant to apply to a sick man. In fact I would have woken the others up and asked for some only I thought it would be selfish to wake them. So I just got up and took my cup and tiptoed out of the Black Hole we slept in, taking great care not to disturb Caspian and Edmund, for they've been sleeping badly since the heat and the short water began. I always try to consider others whether they are nice to me or not. I got out all right into the big room, if you can call it a room, where the rowing benches and the luggage are. The thing of water is at this end. All was going beautifully, but before I'd drawn a cupful who should catch me but that *little spy* Reep. I tried to explain that I was going on deck for a breath of air (the business about the water had nothing to do with him) and he asked me why I had a cup. He made such a noise that the whole ship was roused. They treated me scandalously. I asked, as I think anyone would have, why Reepicheep was sneaking about the water cask in the middle of the night. He said that as he was too small to be any use on deck, he did sentry over the water every night so that one more man could go to sleep. Now comes their rotten unfairness: they all believed *him*. Can you beat it?

"I had to apologize or the dangerous little brute would have been at me with his sword. And then Caspian showed up in his true colors as a brutal tyrant and said out loud for everyone to hear that anyone found 'stealing' water in future would 'get two dozen.' I didn't know what this meant till Edmund explained to me. It comes in the sort of books those Pevensie kids read.

"After this cowardly threat Caspian changed his tune and started being *patronizing*. Said he was sorry for me and that everyone felt just as feverish as I did and we must all make the best of it, etc., etc. Odious stuck-up prig. Stayed in bed all day today.

"*September 7*. A little wind today but still from the west. Made a few miles eastward with part of the sail, set on what Drinian calls the jury-mast— that means the bowsprit set upright and tied (they call it 'lashed') to the stump of the real mast. Still terribly thirsty.

"*September 8*. Still sailing east. I stay in my bunk all day now and see no one except Lucy till the two *fiends* come to bed. Lucy gives me a little of her water ration. She says girls don't get as thirsty as boys. I had often thought this but it ought to be more generally known at sea.

"*September 9*. Land in sight; a very high mountain a long way off to the southeast.

"*September 10*. The mountain is bigger and clearer but still a long way off. Gulls again today for the first time since I don't know how long.

"*September 11*. Caught some fish and had them for dinner. Dropped anchor at about 7 P.M. in three fathoms of water in a bay of this mountainous island. That idiot Caspian wouldn't let us go ashore because it was getting dark and he was afraid of savages and wild beasts. Extra water ration tonight."

What awaited them on this island was going to concern Eustace more than anyone else, but it cannot be told in his words because after September 11 he forgot about keeping his diary for a long time.

When morning came, with a low, gray sky but very hot, the adventurers found they were in a bay encircled by such cliffs and crags that it was like a Norwegian fjord. In front of them, at the head of the bay, there was some level land heavily overgrown with trees that appeared to be cedars, through which a rapid stream came out. Beyond that was a steep ascent ending in a jagged ridge and behind that a vague darkness of mountains

which ran into dull-colored clouds so that you could not see their tops. The nearer cliffs, at each side of the bay, were streaked here and there with lines of white which everyone knew to be waterfalls, though at that distance they did not show any movement or make any noise. Indeed the whole place was very silent and the water of the bay as smooth as glass. It reflected every detail of the cliffs. The scene would have been pretty in a picture but was rather oppressive in real life. It was not a country that welcomed visitors.

The whole ship's company went ashore in two boatloads and everyone drank and washed deliciously in the river and had a meal and a rest before Caspian sent four men back to keep the ship, and the day's work began. There was everything to be done. The casks must be brought ashore and the faulty ones mended if possible and all refilled; a tree—a pine if they could get it—must be felled and made into a new mast; sails must be repaired; a hunting party organized to shoot any game the land might yield; clothes to be washed and mended; and countless small breakages on board to be set right. For the *Dawn Treader* herself—and this was more obvious now that they saw her at a distance—could hardly be recognized as the same gallant ship which had left Narrowhaven. She looked a crippled, discolored hulk which anyone might have taken for a wreck. And her officers and crew were no better—lean, pale, red-eyed from lack of sleep, and dressed in rags.

As Eustace lay under a tree and heard all these plans being discussed his heart sank. Was there going to be no rest? It looked as if their first day on the longed-for land was going to be quite as hard work as a day at sea. Then a delightful idea occurred to him. Nobody was looking—they were all chattering about their ship as if they actually liked the beastly thing. Why shouldn't he simply slip away? He would take a stroll inland, find a cool, airy place up in the mountains, have a good long sleep, and not rejoin the others till the day's work was over. He felt it would do him good. But he would take great care to keep the bay and the ship in sight so as to be sure of his way back. He wouldn't like to be left behind in this country.

He at once put his plan into action. He rose quietly from his place and walked away among the trees, taking care to go slowly and in an aimless manner so that anyone who saw him would think he was merely stretching his legs. He was surprised to find how quickly the noise of conversation died away behind him and how very silent and warm and dark green the wood became. Soon he felt he could venture on a quicker and more determined stride.

This soon brought him out of the wood. The ground began sloping steeply up in front of him.

The grass was dry and slippery but manageable if he used his hands as well as his feet, and though he panted and mopped his forehead a good deal, he plugged away steadily. This showed, by the way, that his new life, little as he suspected it, had already done him some good; the old Eustace, Harold and Alberta's Eustace, would have given up the climb after about ten minutes.

Slowly, and with several rests, he reached the ridge. Here he had expected to have a view into the heart of the island, but the clouds had now come lower and nearer and a sea of fog was rolling to meet him. He sat down and looked back. He was now so high that the bay looked small beneath him and miles of sea were visible. Then the fog from the mountains closed in all round him, thick but not cold, and he lay down and turned this way and that to find the most comfortable position to enjoy himself.

But he didn't enjoy himself, or not for very long. He began, almost for the first time in his life, to feel lonely. At first this feeling grew very gradually. And then he began to worry about the time. There was not the slightest sound. Suddenly it occurred to him that he might have been lying there for hours. Perhaps the others had gone! Perhaps they had let him wander away on purpose simply in order to leave him behind! He leaped up in a panic and began the descent.

At first he tried to do it too quickly, slipped on the steep grass, and slid for several feet. Then he

thought this had carried him too far to the left—and as he came up he had seen precipices on that side. So he clambered up again, as near as he could guess to the place he had started from, and began the descent afresh, bearing to his right. After that things seemed to be going better. He went very cautiously, for he could not see more than a yard ahead, and there was still perfect silence all around him. It is very unpleasant to have to go cautiously when there is a voice inside you saying all the time, "Hurry, hurry, hurry." For every moment the terrible idea of being left behind grew stronger. If he had understood Caspian and the Pevensies at all

he would have known, of course, that there was
not the least chance of their doing any such thing.
But he had persuaded himself that they were all
fiends in human form.

"At last!" said Eustace, as he came slithering
down a slide of loose stones (*scree*, they call it) and
found himself on the level. "And now, where are
those trees? There *is* something dark ahead. Why,
I do believe the fog is clearing."

It was. The light increased every moment and
made him blink. The fog lifted. He was in an ut-
terly unknown valley and the sea was nowhere in
sight.

Six

THE ADVENTURES
OF EUSTACE

AT THAT VERY MOMENT THE OTHERS were washing hands and faces in the river and generally getting ready for dinner and a rest. The three best archers had gone up into the hills north of the bay and returned laden with a pair of wild goats which were now roasting over a fire. Caspian had ordered a cask of wine ashore, strong wine of Archenland which had to be mixed with water before you drank it, so there would be plenty for all. The work had gone well so far and it was a merry meal. Only after the second helping of goat did Edmund say, "Where's that blighter Eustace?"

Meanwhile Eustace stared round the unknown valley. It was so narrow and deep, and the precipices which surrounded it so sheer, that it was like a huge pit or trench. The floor was grassy though strewn with rocks, and here and there Eustace saw black burnt patches like those you see on the sides of a railway embankment in a dry summer. About fifteen yards away from him was a pool of clear, smooth water. There was, at first, nothing else at all in the valley; not an animal, not a bird, not an insect. The sun beat down and grim peaks and horns of mountains peered over the valley's edge.

Eustace realized of course that in the fog he had come down the wrong side of the ridge, so he turned at once to see about getting back. But as soon as he had looked he shuddered. Apparently he had by amazing luck found the only possible way down—a long green spit of land, horribly steep and narrow, with precipices on either side. There was no other possible way of getting back. But could he do it, now that he saw what it was really like? His head swam at the very thought of it.

He turned round again, thinking that at any rate he'd better have a good drink from the pool first. But as soon as he had turned and before he had taken a step forward into the valley he heard a noise behind him. It was only a small noise but it sounded loud in that immense silence. It froze him dead-still where he stood for a second. Then he slewed round his neck and looked.

At the bottom of the cliff a little on his left hand was a low, dark hole—the entrance to a cave perhaps. And out of this two thin wisps of smoke were coming. And the loose stones just beneath the dark hollow were moving (that was the noise he had heard) just as if something were crawling in the dark behind them.

Something *was* crawling. Worse still, something was coming out. Edmund or Lucy or you would have recognized it at once, but Eustace had read none of the right books. The thing that came out of the cave was something he had never even imagined—a long lead-colored snout, dull red eyes, no feathers or fur, a long lithe body that trailed on the ground, legs whose elbows went up higher than its back like a spider's, cruel claws, bat's wings that made a rasping noise on the stones, yards of tail. And the lines of smoke were coming from its two nostrils. He never said the word *Dragon* to himself. Nor would it have made things any better if he had.

But perhaps if he had known something about dragons he would have been a little surprised at this dragon's behavior. It did not sit up and clap its wings, nor did it shoot out a stream of flame from its mouth. The smoke from its nostrils was like the smoke of a fire that will not last much longer. Nor did it seem to have noticed Eustace. It moved very slowly toward the pool—slowly and with many pauses. Even in his fear Eustace felt

that it was an old, sad creature. He wondered if he dared make a dash for the ascent. But it might look round if he made any noise. It might come more to life. Perhaps it was only shamming. Anyway, what was the use of trying to escape by climbing from a creature that could fly?

It reached the pool and slid its horrible scaly

chin down over the gravel to drink: but before it had drunk there came from it a great croaking or clanging cry and after a few twitches and convulsions it rolled round on its side and lay perfectly still with one claw in the air. A little dark blood gushed from its wide-opened mouth. The smoke from its nostrils turned black for a moment and then floated away. No more came.

For a long time Eustace did not dare to move. Perhaps this was the brute's trick, the way it lured travelers to their doom. But one couldn't wait forever. He took a step nearer, then two steps, and halted again. The dragon remained motionless; he noticed too that the red fire had gone out of its eyes. At last he came up to it. He was quite sure now that it was dead. With a shudder he touched it; nothing happened.

The relief was so great that Eustace almost laughed out loud. He began to feel as if he had fought and killed the dragon instead of merely seeing it die. He stepped over it and went to the pool for his drink, for the heat was getting unbearable. He was not surprised when he heard a peal of thunder. Almost immediately afterward the sun disappeared and before he had finished his drink big drops of rain were falling.

The climate of this island was a very unpleasant one. In less than a minute Eustace was wet to the skin and half blinded with such rain as one never sees in Europe. There was no use trying to climb out of the valley as long as this lasted. He bolted for the only shelter in sight—the dragon's cave. There he lay down and tried to get his breath.

Most of us know what we should expect to find in a dragon's lair, but, as I said before, Eustace had read only the wrong books. They had a lot to say about exports and imports and governments and drains, but they were weak on dragons. That is why he was so puzzled at the surface on which he was lying. Parts of it were too prickly to be stones and too hard to be thorns, and there seemed to be a great many round, flat things, and it all clinked when he moved. There was light enough at the cave's mouth to examine it by. And of course Eustace found it to be what any of us could have told him in advance—treasure. There were crowns (those were the prickly things), coins, rings, bracelets, ingots, cups, plates and gems.

Eustace (unlike most boys) had never thought much of treasure but he saw at once the use it would be in this new world which he had so foolishly stumbled into through the picture in Lucy's bedroom at home. "They don't have any tax here," he said, "and you don't have to give treasure to the government. With some of this stuff I could have quite a decent time here—perhaps in Calormen. It sounds the least phony of these countries. I wonder how much I can carry? That bracelet

now—those things in it are probably diamonds—
I'll slip that on my own wrist. Too big, but not if I
push it right up here above my elbow. Then fill
my pockets with diamonds—that's easier than
gold. I wonder when this infernal rain's going to
let up?" He got into a less uncomfortable part of
the pile, where it was mostly coins, and settled
down to wait. But a bad fright, when once it is
over, and especially a bad fright following a mountain walk, leaves you very tired. Eustace fell asleep.

By the time he was sound asleep and snoring
the others had finished dinner and become seriously alarmed about him. They shouted, "Eustace!
Eustace! Coo-ee!" till they were hoarse and
Caspian blew his horn.

"He's nowhere near or he'd have heard that,"
said Lucy with a white face.

"Confound the fellow," said Edmund. "What on
earth did he want to slink away like this for?"

"But we must do something," said Lucy. "He
may have got lost, or fallen into a hole, or been
captured by savages."

"Or killed by wild beasts," said Drinian.

"And a good riddance if he has, *I* say," muttered
Rhince.

"Master Rhince," said Reepicheep, "you never
spoke a word that became you less. The creature is
no friend of mine but he is of the Queen's blood,
and while he is one of our fellowship it concerns

our honor to find him and to avenge him if he is dead."

"Of course we've got to find him (if we *can*)," said Caspian wearily. "That's the nuisance of it. It means a search party and endless trouble. Bother Eustace."

Meanwhile Eustace slept and slept—and slept. What woke him was a pain in his arm. The moon was shining in at the mouth of the cave, and the bed of treasures seemed to have grown much more comfortable: in fact he could hardly feel it at all. He was puzzled by the pain in his arm at first, but presently it occurred to him that the bracelet which he had shoved up above his elbow had become strangely tight. His arm must have swollen while he was asleep (it was his left arm).

He moved his right arm in order to feel his left, but stopped before he had moved it an inch and bit his lip in terror. For just in front of him, and a little on his right, where the moonlight fell clear on the floor of the cave, he saw a hideous shape moving. He knew that shape: it was a dragon's claw. It had moved as he moved his hand and became still when he stopped moving his hand.

"Oh, what a fool I've been," thought Eustace. "Of course, the brute had a mate and it's lying beside me."

For several minutes he did not dare to move a muscle. He saw two thin columns of smoke going up before his eyes, black against the moonlight; just as there had been smoke coming from the other dragon's nose before it died. This was so alarming that he held his breath. The two columns of smoke vanished. When he could hold his breath no longer he let it out stealthily; instantly two jets of smoke appeared again. But even yet he had no idea of the truth.

Presently he decided that he would edge very cautiously to his left and try to creep out of the cave. Perhaps the creature was asleep—and anyway it was his only chance. But of course before he edged to the left he looked to the left. Oh horror! There was a dragon's claw on that side too.

No one will blame Eustace if at this moment he shed tears. He was surprised at the size of his own tears as he saw them splashing on to the treasure in front of him. They also seemed strangely hot; steam went up from them.

But there was no good crying. He must try to crawl out from between the two dragons. He began extending his right arm. The dragon's fore-leg and claw on his right went through exactly the same motion. Then he thought he would try his left. The dragon limb on that side moved too.

Two dragons, one on each side, mimicking whatever he did! His nerve broke and he simply made a bolt for it.

There was such a clatter and rasping, and

clinking of gold, and grinding of stones, as he rushed out of the cave that he thought they were both following him. He daren't look back. He rushed to the pool. The twisted shape of the dead dragon lying in the moonlight would have been enough to frighten anyone but now he hardly noticed it. His idea was to get into the water.

But just as he reached the edge of the pool two things happened. First of all, it came over him like a thunder-clap that he had been running on all fours—and why on earth had he been doing that? And secondly, as he bent toward the water, he thought for a second that yet another dragon was staring up at him out of the pool. But in an instant he realized the truth. The dragon face in the pool was his own reflection. There was no doubt of it. It moved as he moved: it opened and shut its mouth as he opened and shut his.

He had turned into a dragon while he was asleep. Sleeping on a dragon's hoard with greedy, dragonish thoughts in his heart, he had become a dragon himself.

That explained everything. There had been no two dragons beside him in the cave. The claws to right and left had been his own right and left claws. The two columns of smoke had been coming from his own nostrils. As for the pain in his left arm (or what had been his left arm) he could now see what had happened by squinting with his left eye. The bracelet which had fitted very nicely on the upper arm of a boy was far too small for the thick, stumpy foreleg of a dragon. It had sunk deeply into his scaly flesh and there was a throbbing bulge on each side of it. He tore at the place with his dragon's teeth but could not get it off.

In spite of the pain, his first feeling was one of relief. There was nothing to be afraid of any more. He was a terror himself now and nothing in the world but a knight (and not all of those) would dare to attack him. He could get even with Caspian and Edmund now—

But the moment he thought this he realized that he didn't want to. He wanted to be friends. He wanted to get back among humans and talk and laugh and share things. He realized that he was a monster cut off from the whole human race. An appalling loneliness came over him. He began to see that the others had not really been fiends at all. He began to wonder if he himself had been such a nice person as he had always supposed. He longed for their voices. He would have been grateful for a kind word even from Reepicheep.

When he thought of this the poor dragon that had been Eustace lifted up its voice and wept. A powerful dragon crying its eyes out under the moon in a deserted valley is a sight and a sound hardly to be imagined.

At last he decided he would try to find his way

back to the shore. He realized now that Caspian would never have sailed away and left him. And he felt sure that somehow or other he would be able to make people understand who he was.

He took a long drink and then (I know this sounds shocking, but it isn't if you think it over) he ate nearly all the dead dragon. He was half-way through it before he realized what he was doing; for, you see, though his mind was the mind of Eustace, his tastes and his digestion were dragon-ish. And there is nothing a dragon likes so well as fresh dragon. That is why you so seldom find more than one dragon in the same country.

Then he turned to climb out of the valley. He began the climb with a jump and as soon as he jumped he found that he was flying. He had quite forgotten about his wings and it was a great surprise to him—the first pleasant surprise he had had for a long time. He rose high into the air and saw innumerable mountain-tops spread out beneath him in the moonlight. He could see the bay like a silver slab and the *Dawn Treader* lying at anchor and camp fires twinkling in the woods beside the beach. From a great height he launched himself down toward them in a single glide.

Lucy was sleeping very soundly for she had sat up till the return of the search party in hope of good news about Eustace. It had been led by Caspian and had come back late and weary. Their news was disquieting. They had found no trace of Eustace but had seen a dead dragon in a valley. They tried to make the best of it and everyone assured everyone else that there were not likely to be more dragons about, and that one which was dead at about three o'clock that afternoon (which was when they had seen it) would hardly have been killing people a very few hours before.

"Unless it ate the little brat and died of him:

he'd poison anything," said Rhince. But he said this under his breath and no one heard it.

But later in the night Lucy was wakened, very softly, and found the whole company gathered close together and talking in whispers.

"What is it?" said Lucy.

"We must all show great constancy," Caspian was saying. "A dragon has just flown over the tree-tops and lighted on the beach. Yes, I am afraid it is between us and the ship. And arrows are no use against dragons. And they're not at all afraid of fire."

"With your Majesty's leave—" began Reepicheep.

"No, Reepicheep," said the King very firmly, "you are *not* to attempt a single combat with it. And unless you promise to obey me in this matter I'll have you tied up. We must just keep close watch and, as soon as it is light, go down to the beach and give it battle. I will lead. King Edmund will be on my right and the Lord Drinian on my left. There are no other arrangements to be made. It will be light in a couple of hours. In an hour's time let a meal be served out and what is left of the wine. And let everything be done silently."

"Perhaps it will go away," said Lucy.

"It'll be worse if it does," said Edmund, "because then we shan't know where it is. If there's a wasp in the room I like to be able to see it."

The rest of the night was dreadful, and when the meal came, though they knew they ought to eat, many found that they had very poor appetites. And endless hours seemed to pass before the darkness thinned and birds began chirping here and there and the world got colder and wetter than it had been all night and Caspian said, "Now for it, friends."

They got up, all with swords drawn, and formed themselves into a solid mass with Lucy in the middle and Reepicheep on her shoulder. It was nicer than the waiting about and everyone felt fonder of everyone else than at ordinary times. A moment later they were marching. It grew lighter as they came to the edge of the wood. And there on the sand, like a giant lizard, or a flexible crocodile, or a serpent with legs, huge and horrible and humpy, lay the dragon.

But when it saw them, instead of rising up and blowing fire and smoke, the dragon retreated—you could almost say it waddled—back into the shallows of the bay.

"What's it wagging its head like that for?" said Edmund.

"And now it's nodding," said Caspian.

"And there's something coming from its eyes," said Drinian.

"Oh, can't you see," said Lucy. "It's crying. Those are tears."

"I shouldn't trust to that, Ma'am," said Drinian. "That's what crocodiles do, to put you off your guard."

"It wagged its head when you said that," remarked Edmund. "Just as if it meant No. Look, there it goes again."

"Do you think it understands what we're saying?" asked Lucy.

The dragon nodded its head violently.

Reepicheep slipped off Lucy's shoulder and stepped to the front.

"Dragon," came his shrill voice, "can you understand speech?"

The dragon nodded.

"Can you speak?"

It shook its head.

"Then," said Reepicheep, "it is idle to ask you your business. But if you will swear friendship with us raise your left foreleg above your head."

It did so, but clumsily because that leg was sore and swollen with the golden bracelet.

"Oh look," said Lucy, "there's something wrong with its leg. The poor thing—that's probably what it was crying about. Perhaps it came to us to be cured like in Androcles and the lion."

"Be careful, Lucy," said Caspian. "It's a very clever dragon but it may be a liar."

Lucy had, however, already run forward, followed by Reepicheep, as fast as his short legs could carry him, and then of course the boys and Drinian came too.

"Show me your poor paw," said Lucy. "I might be able to cure it."

The dragon-that-had-been-Eustace held out its sore leg gladly enough, remembering how Lucy's cordial had cured him of seasickness before he became a dragon. But he was disappointed. The magic fluid reduced the swelling and eased the pain a little but it could not dissolve the gold.

Everyone had now crowded round to watch the treatment, and Caspian suddenly exclaimed, "Look!" He was staring at the bracelet.

HOW THE
ADVENTURE ENDED

"LOOK AT WHAT?" SAID EDMUND.

"Look at the device on the gold," said Caspian.

"A little hammer with a diamond above it like a star," said Drinian. "Why, I've seen that before."

"Seen it!" said Caspian. "Why, of course you have. It is the sign of a great Narnian house. This is the Lord Octesian's arm-ring."

"Villain," said Reepicheep to the dragon, "have you devoured a Narnian lord?" But the dragon shook his head violently.

"Or perhaps," said Lucy, "this *is* the Lord Octesian, turned into a dragon—under an enchantment, you know."

"It needn't be either," said Edmund. "All dragons collect gold. But I think it's a safe guess that Octesian got no further than this island."

"Are you the Lord Octesian?" said Lucy to the dragon, and then, when it sadly shook its head, "Are you someone enchanted—someone human, I mean?"

It nodded violently.

And then someone said—people disputed afterward whether Lucy or Edmund said it first—"You're not—not Eustace by any chance?"

And Eustace nodded his terrible dragon head and thumped his tail in the sea and everyone skipped back (some of the sailors with ejaculations I will not put down in writing) to avoid the enormous and boiling tears which flowed from his eyes.

Lucy tried hard to console him and even screwed up her courage to kiss the scaly face, and nearly everyone said "Hard luck" and several assured Eustace that they would all stand by him and many said there was sure to be some way of disenchanting him and they'd have him as right as rain in a day or two. And of course they were all very anxious to hear his story, but he couldn't speak. More than once in the days that followed he attempted to write it for them on the sand. But this never succeeded. In the first place Eustace (never having read the right books) had no idea how to tell a story straight. And for another thing, the muscles and nerves of the dragon-claws that he had to use had never learned to write and were not built for writing anyway. As a result he never got nearly to the end before the tide came in and washed away all the writing except the bits he had already trodden on or accidentally swished out with his tail. And all that anyone had seen would be something like this—the dots are for the bits he had smudged out—

 I WNET TO SLEE . . . RGOS AGRONS I MEAN DRANGONS CAVE CAUSE ITWAS DEAD AND AINING SO HAR . . . WOKE UP AND COU . . . GET OFFF MI ARM OH BOTHER . . .

It was, however, clear to everyone that Eustace's character had been rather improved by becoming a dragon. He was anxious to help. He flew over the whole island and found that it was all mountainous and inhabited only by wild goats and droves of wild swine. Of these he brought back many carcasses as provisions for the ship. He was a very humane killer too, for he could dispatch a beast with one blow of his tail so that it didn't know (and presumably still doesn't know) it had been killed. He ate a few himself, of course, but always alone, for now that he was a dragon he liked his food raw but he could never bear to let others see him at his messy meals. And one day, flying slowly and wearily but in great triumph, he bore back to camp a great tall pine tree which he had torn up by the roots in a distant valley and which could be made into a capital mast. And in the evening if it turned chilly, as it sometimes did after the heavy rains, he was a comfort to everyone, for the whole party would come and sit with their backs against his hot sides and get well warmed and dried; and one puff of his fiery breath would light the most obstinate fire. Sometimes he would take a select party for a fly on his back, so that they could see wheeling below them the green slopes, the rocky heights, the narrow pit-like valleys and far out over the sea to the eastward a spot of darker blue on the blue horizon which might be land.

The pleasure (quite new to him) of being liked and, still more, of liking other people, was what kept Eustace from despair. For it was very dreary being a dragon. He shuddered whenever he caught sight of his own reflection as he flew over a mountain lake. He hated the huge bat-like wings, the saw-edged ridge on his back, and the cruel, curved claws. He was almost afraid to be alone with himself and yet he was ashamed to be with the others. On the evenings when he was not being used as a hot-water bottle he would slink away from the camp and lie curled up like a snake between the wood and the water. On such occasions, greatly to his surprise, Reepicheep was his most constant comforter. The noble Mouse would creep away from the merry circle at the camp fire and sit down by the dragon's head, well to the windward to be out of the way of his smoky breath. There he would explain that what had happened to

Eustace was a striking illustration of the turn of
Fortune's wheel, and that if he had Eustace at his
own house in Narnia (it was really a hole not a
house and the dragon's head, let alone his body,
would not have fitted in) he could show him more
than a hundred examples of emperors, kings,
dukes, knights, poets, lovers, astronomers, philoso-
phers, and magicians, who had fallen from prosperity into the most distressing circumstances, and
of whom many had recovered and lived happily
ever afterward. It did not, perhaps, seem so very
comforting at the time, but it was kindly meant
and Eustace never forgot it.

But of course what hung over everyone like a
cloud was the problem of what to do with their
dragon when they were ready to sail. They tried
not to talk of it when he was there, but he couldn't
help overhearing things like, "Would he fit all
along one side of the deck? And we'd have to shift

all the stores to the other side down below so as to balance," or, "Would towing him be any good?" or "Would he be able to keep up by flying?" and (most often of all), "But how are we to feed him?" And poor Eustace realized more and more that since the first day he came on board he had been an unmitigated nuisance and that he was now a greater nuisance still. And this ate into his mind, just as that bracelet ate into his foreleg. He knew that it only made it worse to tear at it with his great teeth, but he couldn't help tearing now and then, especially on hot nights.

About six days after they had landed on Dragon Island, Edmund happened to wake up very early one morning. It was just getting gray so that you could see the tree-trunks if they were between you and the bay but not in the other direction. As he woke he thought he heard something moving, so he raised himself on one elbow and looked about him: and presently he thought he saw a dark figure moving on the seaward side of the wood. The idea that at once occurred to his mind was, "Are we so sure there are no natives on this island after all?" Then he thought it was Caspian—it was about the right size—but he knew that Caspian had been sleeping next to him and could see that he hadn't moved. Edmund made sure that his sword was in its place and then rose to investigate.

He came down softly to the edge of the wood and the dark figure was still there. He saw now that it was too small for Caspian and too big for Lucy. It did not run away. Edmund drew his sword and was about to challenge the stranger when the stranger said in a low voice, "Is that you, Edmund?"

"Yes. Who are you?" said he.

"Don't you know me?" said the other. "It's me—Eustace."

"By jove," said Edmund, "so it is. My dear chap—"

"Hush," said Eustace and lurched as if he were going to fall.

"Hello!" said Edmund, steadying him. "What's up? Are you ill?"

Eustace was silent for so long that Edmund thought he was fainting; but at last he said, "It's been ghastly. You don't know . . . but it's all right now. Could we go and talk somewhere? I don't want to meet the others just yet."

"Yes, rather, anywhere you like," said Edmund. "We can go and sit on the rocks over there. I say, I *am* glad to see you—er—looking yourself again. You must have had a pretty beastly time."

They went to the rocks and sat down looking out across the bay while the sky got paler and paler and the stars disappeared except for one very bright one low down and near the horizon.

"I won't tell you how I became a—a dragon till I can tell the others and get it all over," said Eustace. "By the way, I didn't even know it *was* a dragon till I heard you all using the word when I turned up here the other morning. I want to tell you how I stopped being one."

"Fire ahead," said Edmund.

"Well, last night I was more miserable than ever. And that beastly arm-ring was hurting like anything—"

"Is that all right now?"

Eustace laughed—a different laugh from any Edmund had heard him give before—and slipped the bracelet easily off his arm. "There it is," he said, "and anyone who likes can have it as far as I'm concerned. Well, as I say, I was lying awake and wondering what on earth would become of me. And then—but, mind you, it may have been all a dream. I don't know."

"Go on," said Edmund, with considerable patience.

"Well, anyway, I looked up and saw the very last thing I expected: a huge lion coming slowly toward me. And one queer thing was that there was no moon last night, but there was moonlight where the lion was. So it came nearer and nearer. I was terribly afraid of it. You may think that, being a dragon, I could have knocked any lion out easily enough. But it wasn't that kind of fear. I wasn't afraid of it eating me, I was just afraid of *it*—if you can understand. Well, it came close up to me and looked straight into my eyes. And I shut my eyes tight. But that wasn't any good because it told me to follow it."

"You mean it spoke?"

"I don't know. Now that you mention it, I don't think it did. But it told me all the same. And I knew I'd have to do what it told me, so I got up and followed it. And it led me a long way into the mountains. And there was always this moonlight over and round the lion wherever we went. So at last we came to the top of a mountain I'd never seen before and on the top of this mountain there was a garden—trees and fruit and everything. In the middle of it there was a well.

"I knew it was a well because you could see the water bubbling up from the bottom of it: but it was a lot bigger than most wells—like a very big, round bath with marble steps going down into it. The water was as clear as anything and I thought if I could get in there and bathe it would ease the pain in my leg. But the lion told me I must undress first. Mind you, I don't know if he said any words out loud or not.

"I was just going to say that I couldn't undress because I hadn't any clothes on when I suddenly thought that dragons are snaky sort of things and snakes can cast their skins. Oh, of course, thought I, that's what the lion means. So I started scratching myself and my scales began coming off all over the place. And then I scratched a little deeper and, instead of just scales coming off here and there, my whole skin started peeling off beautifully, like it does after an illness, or as if I was a banana. In a minute or two I just stepped out of it. I could see it lying there beside me, looking rather nasty. It was a most lovely feeling. So I started to go down into the well for my bathe.

"But just as I was going to put my feet into the water I looked down and saw that they were all hard and rough and wrinkled and scaly just as they had been before. Oh, that's all right, said I, it only means I had another smaller suit on underneath the first one, and I'll have to get out of it too. So I scratched and tore again and this underskin peeled off beautifully and out I stepped and left it lying beside the other one and went down to the well for my bathe.

"Well, exactly the same thing happened again. And I thought to myself, oh dear, how ever many skins have I got to take off? For I was longing to bathe my leg. So I scratched away for the third time and got off a third skin, just like the two others, and stepped out of it. But as soon as I looked at myself in the water I knew it had been no good.

"Then the lion said—but I don't know if it spoke—'You will have to let me undress you.' I

was afraid of his claws, I can tell you, but I was
pretty nearly desperate now. So I just lay flat
down on my back to let him do it.

"The very first tear he made was so deep that I
thought it had gone right into my heart. And when
he began pulling the skin off, it hurt worse than
anything I've ever felt. The only thing that made
me able to bear it was just the pleasure of feeling
the stuff peel off. You know—if you've ever picked
the scab of a sore place. It hurts like billy-oh but it
is such fun to see it coming away."

"I know exactly what you mean," said Edmund.

"Well, he peeled the beastly stuff right off—just
as I thought I'd done it myself the other three
times, only they hadn't hurt—and there it was lying
on the grass: only ever so much thicker, and darker,
and more knobbly-looking than the others had been.
And there was I as smooth and soft as a peeled
switch and smaller than I had been. Then he caught
hold of me—I didn't like that much for I was very
tender underneath now that I'd no skin on—and
threw me into the water. It smarted like anything
but only for a moment. After that it became perfectly delicious and as soon as I started swimming
and splashing I found that all the pain had gone
from my arm. And then I saw why. I'd turned into
a boy again. You'd think me simply phony if I told
you how I felt about my own arms. I know they've
no muscle and are pretty mouldy compared with

Caspian's, but I was so glad to see them.

"After a bit the lion took me out and dressed me—"

"Dressed you. With his paws?"

"Well, I don't exactly remember that bit. But he did somehow or other: in new clothes—the same I've got on now, as a matter of fact. And then suddenly I was back here. Which is what makes me think it must have been a dream."

"No. It wasn't a dream," said Edmund.

"Why not?"

"Well, there are the clothes, for one thing. And you have been—well, un-dragoned, for another."

"What do you think it was, then?" asked Eustace.

"I think you've seen Aslan," said Edmund.

"Aslan!" said Eustace. "I've heard that name mentioned several times since we joined the *Dawn Treader*. And I felt—I don't know what—I hated it. But I was hating everything then. And by the way, I'd like to apologize. I'm afraid I've been pretty beastly."

"That's all right," said Edmund. "Between ourselves, you haven't been as bad as I was on my first trip to Narnia. You were only an ass, but I was a traitor."

"Well, don't tell me about it, then," said Eustace. "But who is Aslan? Do you know him?"

"Well—he knows me," said Edmund. "He is the

great Lion, the son of the Emperor-beyond-the-Sea, who saved me and saved Narnia. We've all seen him. Lucy sees him most often. And it may be Aslan's country we are sailing to."

Neither said anything for a while. The last bright star had vanished and though they could not see the sunrise because of the mountains on their right, they knew it was going on because the sky above them and the bay before them turned the color of roses. Then some bird of the parrot kind screamed in the wood behind them, they heard movements among the trees, and finally a blast on Caspian's horn. The camp was astir.

Great was the rejoicing when Edmund and the restored Eustace walked into the breakfast circle round the camp fire. And now of course everyone heard the earlier part of his story. People wondered whether the other dragon had killed the Lord Octesian several years ago or whether Octesian himself had been the old dragon. The jewels with which Eustace had crammed his pockets in the cave had disappeared along with the clothes he had then been wearing: but no one, least of all Eustace himself, felt any desire to go back to that valley for more treasure.

In a few days now the *Dawn Treader*, remasted, repainted, and well stored, was ready to sail. Before they embarked Caspian caused to be cut on a smooth cliff facing the bay the words:

DRAGON ISLAND
DISCOVERED BY CASPIAN X, KING OF NARNIA, ETC.
IN THE FOURTH
YEAR OF HIS REIGN.
HERE, AS WE SUPPOSE, THE LORD OCTESIAN
HAD HIS DEATH

It would be nice, and fairly nearly true, to say that "from that time forth Eustace was a different boy." To be strictly accurate, he began to be a different boy. He had relapses. There were still many days when he could be very tiresome. But most of those I shall not notice. The cure had begun.

The Lord Octesian's arm ring had a curious fate. Eustace did not want it and offered it to Caspian and Caspian offered it to Lucy. She did not care about having it. "Very well, then, catch as catch can," said Caspian and flung it up in the air. This was when they were all standing looking at the inscription. Up went the ring, flashing in the sunlight, and caught, and hung, as neatly as a well-thrown quoit, on a little projection on the rock. No one could climb up to get it from below and no one could climb down to get it from above. And there, for all I know, it is hanging still and may hang till that world ends.

Eight

TWO NARROW ESCAPES

EVERYONE WAS CHEERFUL AS THE *DAWN Treader* sailed from Dragon Island. They had fair winds as soon as they were out of the bay and came early next morning to the unknown land which some of them had seen when flying over the mountains while Eustace was still a dragon. It was a low green island inhabited by nothing but rabbits and a few goats, but from the ruins of stone huts, and from blackened places where fires had been, they judged that it had been peopled not long before. There were also some bones and broken weapons.

"Pirates' work," said Caspian.

"Or the dragon's," said Edmund.

The only other thing they found here was a little skin boat, or coracle, on the sands. It was made of hide stretched over a wicker framework. It was a tiny boat, barely four feet long, and the paddle which still lay in it was in proportion. They thought that either it had been made for a child or else that the people of that country had been Dwarfs. Reepicheep decided to keep it, as it was just the right size for him; so it was taken on board. They called that land Burnt Island, and sailed away before noon.

For some five days they ran before a south-southeast wind, out of sight of all lands and seeing neither fish nor gull. Then they had a day that rained hard till the afternoon. Eustace lost two games of chess to Reepicheep and began to get like his old and disagreeable self again, and Edmund said he wished they could have gone to America with Susan. Then Lucy looked out of the stern windows and said:

"Hello! I do believe it's stopping. And what's *that?*"

They all tumbled up to the poop at this and found that the rain had stopped and that Drinian, who was on watch, was also staring hard at something astern. Or rather, at several things. They looked a little like smooth rounded rocks, a whole line of them with intervals of about forty feet in between.

"But they can't be rocks," Drinian was saying, "because they weren't there five minutes ago."

"And one's just disappeared," said Lucy.

"Yes, and there's another one coming up," said Edmund.

"And nearer," said Eustace.

"Hang it!" said Caspian. "The whole thing is moving this way."

"And moving a great deal quicker than we can sail, Sire," said Drinian. "It'll be up with us in a minute."

They all held their breath, for it is not at all nice to be pursued by an unknown something either on land or sea. But what it turned out to be was far worse than anyone had suspected. Suddenly, only about the length of a cricket pitch from their port side, an appalling head reared itself out of the sea. It was all greens and vermilions with purple blotches—except where shellfish clung to it—and shaped rather like a horse's, though without ears. It had enormous eyes, eyes made for staring through the dark depths of the ocean, and a gaping mouth filled with double rows of sharp fish-like teeth. It came up on what they first took to be a huge neck, but as more and more of it emerged everyone knew that this was not its neck but its body and that at last they were seeing what so many people have foolishly wanted to see—the great Sea Serpent. The folds of its gigantic tail could be seen far away, rising at intervals from the surface. And now its head was towering up higher than the mast.

Every man rushed to his weapon, but there was nothing to be done, the monster was out of reach. "Shoot! Shoot!" cried the Master Bowman, and several obeyed, but the arrows glanced off the Sea Serpent's hide as if it was iron-plated. Then, for a dreadful minute, everyone was still, staring up at its eyes and mouth and wondering where it would pounce.

But it didn't pounce. It shot its head forward across the ship on a level with the yard of the mast. Now its head was just beside the fighting-top. Still it stretched and stretched till its head was over the starboard bulwark. Then down it began to come—not onto the crowded deck but into the water, so that the whole ship was under an arch of serpent. And almost at once that arch began to get smaller: indeed on the starboard the Sea Serpent was now almost touching the *Dawn Treader*'s side.

Eustace (who had really been trying very hard to behave well, till the rain and the chess put him back) now did the first brave thing he had ever done. He was wearing a sword that Caspian had lent him. As soon as the serpent's body was near enough on the starboard side he jumped on to the bulwark and began hacking at it with all his might. It is true that he accomplished nothing beyond breaking Caspian's second-best sword into bits, but it was a fine thing for a beginner to have done.

Others would have joined him if at that moment Reepicheep had not called out, "Don't fight! Push!" It was so unusual for the Mouse to advise anyone not to fight that, even in that terrible moment, every eye turned to him. And when he jumped up on to the bulwark, forward of the snake, and set his little furry back against its huge scaly, slimy back, and began pushing as hard as he could, quite a number of people saw what he meant and rushed to both sides of the ship to do the same. And when, a moment later, the Sea Serpent's head appeared again, this time on the port side, and this time with its back to them, then everyone understood.

The brute had made a loop of itself round the *Dawn Treader* and was beginning to draw the loop tight. When it got quite tight—snap!—there would be floating matchwood where the ship had been and it could pick them out of the water one by one. Their only chance was to push the loop backward till it slid over the stern; or else (to put the same thing another way) to push the ship forward out of the loop.

Reepicheep alone had, of course, no more chance of doing this than of lifting up a cathedral, but he had nearly killed himself with trying before others shoved him aside. Very soon the whole ship's company except Lucy and the Mouse (which was fainting) was in two long lines along the two bulwarks, each man's chest to the back of the man in front, so that the weight of the whole line was in the last man, pushing for their lives. For a few sickening seconds (which seemed like hours) nothing appeared to happen. Joints cracked, sweat dropped, breath came in grunts and gasps. Then they felt that the ship was moving. They saw that the snake-loop was further from the mast than it had been. But they also saw that it was smaller. And now the real danger was at hand. Could they get it over the poop, or was it already too tight? Yes. It would just fit. It was resting on the poop rails. A dozen or more sprang up on the poop. This was far better. The Sea Serpent's body was so low now that they could make a line across the poop and push side by side. Hope rose high till everyone remembered the high carved stern, the dragon tail, of the *Dawn Treader*. It would be quite impossible to get the brute over that.

"An axe," cried Caspian hoarsely, "and still shove." Lucy, who knew where everything was, heard him where she was standing on the main deck staring up at the poop. In a few seconds she had been below, got the axe, and was rushing up the ladder to the poop. But just as she reached the top there came a great crashing noise like a tree coming down and the ship rocked and darted forward. For at that very moment, whether because the Sea Serpent was being pushed so hard, or because it foolishly decided to draw the noose tight, the whole of the carved stern broke off and the ship was free.

The others were too exhausted to see what Lucy saw. There, a few yards behind them, the loop of Sea Serpent's body got rapidly smaller and disappeared into a splash. Lucy always said (but of course she was very excited at the moment, and it may have been only imagination) that she saw a look of idiotic satisfaction on the creature's face. What is certain is that it was a very stupid animal, for instead of pursuing the ship it turned its head round and began nosing all along its own body as if it expected to find the wreckage of the *Dawn Treader* there. But the *Dawn Treader* was already well away, running before a fresh breeze, and the men lay and sat panting and groaning all about the deck, till presently they were able to talk about it, and then to laugh about it. And when some rum had been served out they even raised a cheer; and everyone praised the valor of Eustace (though it hadn't done any good) and of Reepicheep.

After this they sailed for three days more and saw nothing but sea and sky. On the fourth day the wind changed to the north and the seas began to rise; by the afternoon it had nearly become a gale. But at the same time they sighted land on their port bow.

"By your leave, Sire," said Drinian, "we will try to get under the lee of that country by rowing and lie in harbor, maybe till this is over." Caspian agreed, but a long row against the gale did not bring them to the land before evening. By the last light of that day they steered into a natural harbor and anchored, but no one went ashore that night. In the morning they found themselves in the green bay of a rugged, lonely-looking country which sloped up to a rocky summit. From the windy north beyond that summit clouds came streaming rapidly. They lowered the boat and loaded her with any of the water casks which were now empty.

"Which stream shall we water at, Drinian?" said Caspian as he took his seat in the stern-sheets of the boat. "There seem to be two coming down into the bay."

"It makes little odds, Sire," said Drinian. "But I think it's a shorter pull to that on the starboard— the eastern one."

"Here comes the rain," said Lucy.

"I should think it does!" said Edmund, for it was already pelting hard. "I say, let's go to the other stream. There are trees there and we'll have some shelter."

"Yes, let's," said Eustace. "No point in getting wetter than we need."

But all the time Drinian was steadily steering to the starboard, like tiresome people in cars who continue at forty miles an hour while you are explaining to them that they are on the wrong road.

"They're right, Drinian," said Caspian. "Why don't you bring her head round and make for the western stream?"

"As your Majesty pleases," said Drinian a little shortly. He had had an anxious day with the weather yesterday, and he didn't like advice from landsmen. But he altered course; and it turned out afterward that it was a good thing he did.

By the time they had finished watering, the rain was over and Caspian, with Eustace, the Pevensies, and Reepicheep, decided to walk up to the top of the hill and see what could be seen. It was a stiffish climb through coarse grass and heather and they saw neither man nor beast, except seagulls. When they reached the top they saw that it was a very small island, not more than twenty acres; and from this height the sea looked larger and more desolate than it did from the deck, or even the fighting-top, of the *Dawn Treader*.

"Crazy, you know," said Eustace to Lucy in a low voice, looking at the eastern horizon. "Sailing on and on into *that* with no idea what we may get to." But he only said it out of habit, not really nastily as he would have done at one time.

It was too cold to stay long on the ridge for the wind still blew freshly from the north.

"Don't let's go back the same way," said Lucy as they turned; "let's go along a bit and come down by the other stream, the one Drinian wanted to go to."

Everyone agreed to this and after about fifteen minutes they were at the source of the second river. It was a more interesting place than they had expected; a deep little mountain lake, surrounded by cliffs except for a narrow channel on the seaward side out of which the water flowed.

Here at last they were out of the wind, and all sat down in the heather above the cliff for a rest.

All sat down, but one (it was Edmund) jumped up again very quickly.

"They go in for sharp stones on this island," he said, groping about in the heather. "Where is the wretched thing? . . . Ah, now I've got it . . . Hullo! It wasn't a stone at all, it's a sword-hilt. No, by jove, it's a whole sword; what the rust has left of it. It must have lain here for ages."

"Narnian, too, by the look of it," said Caspian, as they all crowded round.

"I'm sitting on something too," said Lucy. "Something hard." It turned out to be the remains of a mail shirt. By this time everyone was on hands and knees, feeling in the thick heather in every direction. Their search revealed, one by one, a helmet, a dagger, and a few coins; not Calormen crescents but genuine Narnian "Lions" and "Trees" such as you might see any day in the market-place of Beaversdam or Beruna.

"Looks as if this might be all that's left of one of our seven lords," said Edmund.

"Just what I was thinking," said Caspian. "I wonder which it was. There's nothing on the dagger to show. And I wonder how he died."

"And how we are to avenge him," added Reepicheep.

Edmund, the only one of the party who had read several detective stories, had meanwhile been thinking.

"Look here," he said, "there's something very fishy about this. He can't have been killed in a fight."

"Why not?" asked Caspian.

"No bones," said Edmund. "An enemy might take the armor and leave the body. But who ever heard of a chap who'd won a fight carrying away the body and leaving the armor?"

"Perhaps he was killed by a wild animal," Lucy suggested.

"It'd be a clever animal," said Edmund, "that would take a man's mail shirt off."

"Perhaps a dragon?" said Caspian.

"Nothing doing," said Eustace. "A dragon couldn't do it. I ought to know."

"Well, let's get away from the place, anyway," said Lucy. She had not felt like sitting down again since Edmund had raised the question of bones.

"If you like," said Caspian, getting up. "I don't think any of this stuff is worth taking away."

They came down and round to the little opening where the stream came out of the lake, and stood looking at the deep water within the circle of cliffs. If it had been a hot day, no doubt some would have been tempted to bathe and everyone would have had a drink. Indeed, even as it was, Eustace was on the very point of stooping down and scooping up some water in his hands when Reepicheep and Lucy both at the same moment cried, "Look," so he forgot about his drink and looked into the water.

The bottom of the pool was made of large grayish-blue stones and the water was perfectly clear, and on the bottom lay a life-size figure of a man, made apparently of gold. It lay face downward with its arms stretched out above its head. And it so happened that as they looked at it, the clouds parted and the sun shone out. The golden shape was lit up from end to end. Lucy thought it was the most beautiful statue she had ever seen.

"Well!" whistled Caspian. "That was worth coming to see! I wonder, can we get it out?"

"We can dive for it, Sire," said Reepicheep.

"No good at all," said Edmund. "At least, if it's really gold—solid gold—it'll be far too heavy to bring up. And that pool's twelve or fifteen feet deep if it's an inch. Half a moment, though. It's a good thing I've brought a hunting spear with me. Let's see what the depth *is* like. Hold on to my hand, Caspian, while I lean out over the water a bit." Caspian took his hand and Edmund, leaning forward, began to lower his spear into the water.

Before it was half-way in Lucy said, "I don't believe the statue is gold at all. It's only the light. Your spear looks just the same color."

"What's wrong?" asked several voices at once;

for Edmund had suddenly let go of the spear.

"I couldn't hold it," gasped Edmund. "It seemed so *heavy*."

"And there it is on the bottom now," said Caspian, "and Lucy is right. It looks just the same color as the statue."

But Edmund, who appeared to be having some trouble with his boots—at least he was bending down and looking at them—straightened himself all at once and shouted out in the sharp voice which people hardly ever disobey:

"Get back! Back from the water. All of you. At once!!"

They all did and stared at him.

"Look," said Edmund, "look at the toes of my boots."

"They look a bit yellow," began Eustace.

"They're gold, solid gold," interrupted Edmund. "Look at them. Feel them. The leather's pulled away from it already. And they're as heavy as lead."

"By Aslan!" said Caspian. "You don't mean to say—?"

"Yes, I do," said Edmund. "That water turns things into gold. It turned the spear into gold, that's why it got so heavy. And it was just lapping against my feet (it's a good thing I wasn't barefoot) and it turned the toe-caps into gold. And that poor fellow on the bottom—well, you see."

"So it isn't a statue at all," said Lucy in a low voice.

"No. The whole thing is plain now. He was here on a hot day. He undressed on top of the cliff—where we were sitting. The clothes have rotted away or been taken by birds to line nests with; the armor's still there. Then he dived and—"

"Don't," said Lucy. "What a horrible thing."

"And what a narrow shave *we've* had," said Edmund.

"Narrow indeed," said Reepicheep. "Anyone's finger, anyone's foot, anyone's whisker, or anyone's tail, might have slipped into the water at any moment."

"All the same," said Caspian, "we may as well test it." He stooped down and wrenched up a spray of heather. Then, very cautiously, he knelt beside the pool and dipped it in. It was heather that he dipped; what he drew out was a perfect model of heather made of the purest gold, heavy and soft as lead.

"The King who owned this island," said Caspian

slowly, and his face flushed as he spoke, "would soon be the richest of all Kings of the world. I claim this land forever as a Narnian possession. It shall be called Goldwater Island. And I bind all of you to secrecy. No one must know of this. Not even Drinian—on pain of death, do you hear?"

"Who are you talking to?" said Edmund. "I'm no subject of yours. If anything it's the other way round. I am one of the four ancient sovereigns of Narnia and you are under allegiance to the High King my brother."

"So it has come to that, King Edmund, has it?" said Caspian, laying his hand on his sword-hilt.

"Oh, stop it, both of you," said Lucy. "That's the worst of doing anything with boys. You're all such swaggering, bullying idiots—oooh!—" Her voice died away into a gasp. And everyone else saw what she had seen.

Across the gray hillside above them—gray, for the heather was not yet in bloom—without noise, and without looking at them, and shining as if he were in bright sunlight though the sun had in fact gone in, passed with slow pace the hugest lion that human eyes have ever seen. In describing the scene Lucy said afterward, "He was the size of an elephant," though at another time she only said, "The size of a cart-horse." But it was not the size that mattered. Nobody dared to ask what it was. They knew it was Aslan.

And nobody ever saw how or where he went. They looked at one another like people waking from sleep.

"What were we talking about?" said Caspian. "Have I been making rather an ass of myself?"

"Sire," said Reepicheep, "this is a place with a curse on it. Let us get back on board at once. And if I might have the honor of naming this island, I should call it Deathwater."

"That strikes me as a very good name, Reep," said Caspian, "though now that I come to think of it, I don't know why. But the weather seems to be settling and I dare say Drinian would like to be off. What a lot we shall have to tell him."

But in fact they had not much to tell for the memory of the last hour had all become confused.

"Their Majesties all seemed a bit bewitched when they came aboard," said Drinian to Rhince some hours later when the *Dawn Treader* was once more under sail and Deathwater Island already below the horizon. "Something happened to them in that place. The only thing I could get clear was that they think they've found the body of one of these lords we're looking for."

"You don't say so, Captain," answered Rhince. "Well, that's three. Only four more. At this rate we might be home soon after the New Year. And a good thing too. My baccy's running a bit low. Good night, Sir."

THE ISLAND
OF THE VOICES

AND NOW THE WINDS WHICH HAD SO long been from the northwest began to blow from the west itself and every morning when the sun rose out of the sea the curved prow of the *Dawn Treader* stood up right across the middle of the sun. Some thought that the sun looked larger than it looked from Narnia, but others disagreed. And they sailed and sailed before a gentle yet steady breeze and saw neither fish nor gull nor ship nor shore. And stores began to get low again, and it crept into their hearts that perhaps they might have come to a sea which went on forever. But when the very last day on which they thought they could risk continuing their eastward voyage dawned, it revealed, right ahead between them and the sunrise, a low land lying like a cloud.

They made harbor in a wide bay about the middle of the afternoon and landed. It was a very different country from any they had yet seen. For when they had crossed the sandy beach they found all silent and empty as if it were an uninhabited land, but before them there were level lawns in which the grass was as smooth and short as it used to be in the grounds of a great English house where ten gardeners were kept. The trees, of which there were many, all stood well apart from one another, and there were no broken branches and no leaves lying on the ground. Pigeons sometimes cooed but there was no other noise.

Presently they came to a long, straight, sanded path with not a weed growing on it and trees on either hand. Far off at the other end of this avenue they now caught sight of a house—very long and gray and quiet-looking in the afternoon sun.

Almost as soon as they entered this path Lucy noticed that she had a little stone in her shoe. In that unknown place it might have been wiser for her to ask the others to wait while she took it out. But she didn't; she just dropped quietly behind and sat down to take off her shoe. Her lace had got into a knot.

Before she had undone the knot the others were a fair distance ahead. By the time she had got the stone out and was putting the shoe on again she could no longer hear them. But almost at once she heard something else. It was not coming from the direction of the house.

What she heard was a thumping. It sounded as

if dozens of strong workmen were hitting the ground as hard as they could with great wooden mallets. And it was very quickly coming nearer. She was already sitting with her back to a tree, and as the tree was not one she could climb, there was really nothing to do but to sit dead still and press herself against the tree and hope she wouldn't be seen.

Thump, thump, thump . . . and whatever it was must be very close now for she could feel the ground shaking. But she could see nothing. She thought the thing—or things—must be just behind her. But then there came a thump on the path right in front of her. She knew it was on the path not only by the sound but because she saw the sand scatter as if it had been struck a heavy blow. But she could see nothing that had struck it. Then all the thumping noises drew together about twenty feet away from her and suddenly ceased. Then came the Voice.

It was really very dreadful because she could still see nobody at all. The whole of that park-like country still looked as quiet and empty as it had looked when they first landed. Nevertheless, only a few feet away from her, a voice spoke. And what it said was:

"Mates, now's our chance."

Instantly a whole chorus of other voices replied, "Hear him. Hear him. 'Now's our chance,' he said. Well done, Chief. You never said a truer word."

"What I say," continued the first voice, "is, get down to the shore between them and their boat, and let every mother's son look to his weapons. Catch 'em when they try to put to sea."

"Eh, that's the way," shouted all the other voices. "You never made a better plan, Chief. Keep it up, Chief. You couldn't have a better plan than that."

"Lively, then, mates, lively," said the first voice. "Off we go."

"Right again, Chief," said the others. "Couldn't have a better order. Just what we were going to say ourselves. Off we go."

Immediately the thumping began again—very

loud at first but soon fainter and fainter, till it died out in the direction of the sea.

Lucy knew there was no time to sit puzzling as to what these invisible creatures might be. As soon as the thumping noise had died away she got up and ran along the path after the others as quickly as her legs would carry her. They must at all costs be warned.

While this had been happening the others had reached the house. It was a low building—only two stories high—made of a beautiful mellow stone, many-windowed, and partially covered with ivy. Everything was so still that Eustace said, "I think it's empty," but Caspian silently pointed to the column of smoke which rose from one chimney.

They found a wide gateway open and passed through it into a paved courtyard. And it was here that they had their first indication that there was something odd about this island. In the middle of the courtyard stood a pump, and beneath the pump a bucket. There was nothing odd about that. But the pump handle was moving up and down, though there seemed to be no one moving it.

"There's some magic at work here," said Caspian.

"Machinery!" said Eustace. "I do believe we've come to a civilized country at last."

At that moment Lucy, hot and breathless, rushed into the courtyard behind them. In a low voice she tried to make them understand what she had overheard. And when they had partly understood it even the bravest of them did not look very happy.

"Invisible enemies," muttered Caspian. "And cutting us off from the boat. This is an ugly furrow to plow."

"You've no idea what *sort* of creatures they are, Lu?" asked Edmund.

"How can I, Ed, when I couldn't see them?"

"Did they sound like humans from their footsteps?"

"I didn't hear any noise of feet—only voices and this frightful thudding and thumping—like a mallet."

"I wonder," said Reepicheep, "do they become

visible when you drive a sword into them?"

"It looks as if we shall find out," said Caspian. "But let's get out of this gateway. There's one of these gentry at that pump listening to all we say."

They came out and went back on to the path where the trees might possibly make them less conspicuous. "Not that it's any good *really*," said Eustace, "trying to hide from people you can't see. They may be all round us."

"Now, Drinian," said Caspian. "How would it be if we gave up the boat for lost, went down to another part of the bay, and signaled to the *Dawn Treader* to stand in and take us aboard?"

"Not depth for her, Sire," said Drinian.

"We could swim," said Lucy.

"Your Majesties all," said Reepicheep, "hear me. It is folly to think of avoiding an invisible enemy by any amount of creeping and skulking. If these creatures mean to bring us to battle, be sure they will succeed. And whatever comes of it I'd sooner meet them face to face than be caught by the tail."

"I really think Reep is in the right this time," said Edmund.

"Surely," said Lucy, "if Rhince and the others on the *Dawn Treader* see us fighting on the shore they'll be able to do *something*."

"But they won't see us fighting if they can't see any enemy," said Eustace miserably. "They'll think we're just swinging our swords in the air for fun."

There was an uncomfortable pause.

"Well," said Caspian at last, "let's get on with it. We must go and face them. Shake hands all round—arrow on the string, Lucy—swords out, everyone else—and now for it. Perhaps they'll parley."

It was strange to see the lawns and the great trees looking so peaceful as they marched back to the beach. And when they arrived there, and saw the boat lying where they had left her, and the smooth sand with no one to be seen on it, more than one doubted whether Lucy had not merely imagined all she had told them. But before they reached the sand, a voice spoke out of the air.

"No further, masters, no further now," it said. "We've got to talk with you first. There's fifty of us and more here with weapons in our fists."

"Hear him, hear him," came the chorus. "That's our Chief. You can depend on what he says. He's telling you the truth, he is."

"I do not see these fifty warriors," observed Reepicheep.

"That's right, that's right," said the Chief Voice. "You don't see us. And why not? Because we're invisible."

"Keep it up, Chief, keep it up," said the Other Voices. "You're talking like a book. They couldn't ask for a better answer than that."

"Be quiet, Reep," said Caspian, and then added

in a louder voice, "You invisible people, what do you want with us? And what have we done to earn your enmity?"

"We want something that little girl can do for us," said the Chief Voice. (The others explained that this was just what they would have said themselves.)

"Little girl!" said Reepicheep. "The lady is a queen."

"We don't know about queens," said the Chief Voice. ("No more we do, no more we do," chimed in the others.) "But we want something she can do."

"What is it?" said Lucy.

"And if it is anything against her Majesty's honor or safety," added Reepicheep, "you will wonder to see how many we can kill before we die."

"Well," said the Chief Voice. "It's a long story. Suppose we all sit down?"

The proposal was warmly approved by the other voices but the Narnians remained standing.

"Well," said the Chief Voice. "It's like this. This island has been the property of a great magician time out of mind. And we all are—or perhaps in a manner of speaking, I might say, we were—his servants. Well, to cut a long story short, this magician that I was speaking about, he told us to do something we didn't like. And why not? Because we didn't want to. Well, then, this same magician he fell into a great rage; for I ought to tell you he owned the island and he wasn't used to being crossed. He was terribly downright, you know. But let me see, where am I? Oh yes, this magician then, he goes upstairs (for you must know he kept all his magic things up there and we all lived down below), I say he goes upstairs and puts a spell on us. An uglifying spell. If you saw us now, which in my opinion you may thank your stars you can't, you wouldn't believe what we looked like before we were uglified. You wouldn't really. So there we all were so ugly we couldn't bear to look at one another. So then what did we do? Well, I'll tell you what we did. We waited till we thought this same magician would be asleep in the afternoon and we creep upstairs and go to his magic book, as bold as brass, to see if we can do anything about this uglification. But we were all of a sweat and a tremble, so I won't deceive you. But, believe me or believe me not, I do assure you that we couldn't find anything in the way of a spell for taking off the ugliness. And what with time getting on and being afraid that the old gentleman might wake up any minute—I was all of a muck sweat, so I won't deceive you—well, to cut a long story short, whether we did right or whether we did wrong, in the end we see a spell for making people invisible. And we thought we'd rather be invisible than go on being as ugly as all that. And why? Because we'd like it better. So my little girl, who's just about your little girl's age, and a sweet child she was before she was uglified, though now—but least said soonest mended—I say, my little girl she says the spell, for it's got to be a little girl or else the magician himself, if you see my meaning, for otherwise it won't work. And why not? Because nothing happens. So my Clipsie says the spell, for I ought to have told you she reads beautifully, and there we all were as invisible as you could wish to see. And I do assure you it was a relief not to see one another's faces. At first, anyway. But the long and the short of it is we're mortal tired of being invisible. And there's another thing. We never reckoned on this magician (the one I was telling you about before) going invisible too. But we haven't ever seen him since. So we don't know if he's dead, or gone away, or whether he's just sitting upstairs being invisible, and perhaps coming down and being invisible there. And, believe me, it's no manner of use listening because he always did go about with his bare feet on, making no more noise than a great big cat. And I'll tell all you gentlemen straight, it's getting more than what our nerves can stand."

Such was the Chief Voice's story, but very much shortened, because I have left out what the Other Voices said. Actually he never got out more than six or seven words without being interrupted by their agreements and encouragements, which drove the Narnians nearly out of their minds with impatience. When it was over there was a very long silence.

"But," said Lucy at last, "what's all this got to do with us? I don't understand."

"Why, bless me, if I haven't gone and left out the whole point," said the Chief Voice.

"That you have, that you have," roared the Other Voices with great enthusiasm. "No one couldn't have left it out cleaner and better. Keep it up, Chief, keep it up."

"Well, I needn't go over the whole story again," began the Chief Voice.

"No. Certainly not," said Caspian and Edmund.

"Well, then, to put it in a nutshell," said the Chief Voice, "we've been waiting for ever so long for a nice little girl from foreign parts, like it might be you, Missie—that would go upstairs and go to the magic book and find the spell that takes off the invisibleness, and say it. And we all swore that the first strangers as landed on this island (having a nice little girl with them, I mean, for if they hadn't it'd be another matter) we wouldn't let them go away alive unless they'd done the needful for us. And that's why, gentlemen, if your little girl doesn't come up to scratch, it will be our painful duty to cut all your throats. Merely in the way of business, as you might say, and no offense, I hope."

"I don't see all your weapons," said Reepicheep.

"Are they invisible too?" The words were scarcely out of his mouth before they heard a whizzing sound and next moment a spear had stuck, quivering, in one of the trees behind them.

"That's a spear, that is," said the Chief Voice.

"That it is, Chief, that it is," said the others. "You couldn't have put it better."

"And it came from my hand," the Chief Voice continued. "They get visible when they leave us."

"But why do you want *me* to do this?" asked Lucy. "Why can't one of your own people? Haven't you got any girls?"

"We dursen't, we dursen't," said all the Voices. "We're not going upstairs again."

"In other words," said Caspian, "you are asking this lady to face some danger which you daren't ask your own sisters and daughters to face!"

"That's right, that's right," said all the Voices cheerfully. "You couldn't have said it better. Eh, you've had some education, you have. Anyone can see that."

"Well, of all the outrageous—" began Edmund, but Lucy interrupted.

"Would I have to go upstairs at night, or would it do in daylight?"

"Oh, daylight, daylight, to be sure," said the Chief Voice. "Not at night. No one's asking you to do that. Go upstairs in the dark? Ugh."

"All right, then, I'll do it," said Lucy. "No," she

said, turning to the others, "don't try to stop me. Can't you see it's no use? There are dozens of them there. We can't fight them. And the other way there *is* a chance."

"But a magician!" said Caspian.

"I know," said Lucy. "But he mayn't be as bad as they make out. Don't you get the idea that these people are not very brave?"

"They're certainly not very clever," said Eustace.

"Look here, Lu," said Edmund. "We really can't let you do a thing like this. Ask Reep, I'm sure he'll say just the same."

"But it's to save my own life as well as yours," said Lucy. "I don't want to be cut to bits with invisible swords any more than anyone else."

"Her Majesty is in the right," said Reepicheep. "If we had any assurance of saving *her* by battle, our duty would be very plain. It appears to me that we have none. And the service they ask of her is in no way contrary to her Majesty's honor, but a noble and heroical act. If the Queen's heart moves her to risk the magician, I will not speak against it."

As no one had ever known Reepicheep to be afraid of anything, he could say this without feeling at all awkward. But the boys, who had all been afraid quite often, grew very red. None the less, it was such obvious sense that they had to give in. Loud cheers broke from the invisible people when their decision was announced, and the Chief Voice (warmly supported by all the others) invited the Narnians to come to supper and spend the night. Eustace didn't want to accept, but Lucy said, "I'm sure they're not treacherous. They're not like that at all," and the others agreed. And so, accompanied by an enormous noise of thumpings (which became louder when they reached the flagged and echoing courtyard) they all went back to the house.

THE MAGICIAN'S BOOK

THE INVISIBLE PEOPLE FEASTED THEIR guests royally. It was very funny to see the plates and dishes coming to the table and not to see anyone carrying them. It would have been funny even if they had moved along level with the floor, as you would expect things to do in invisible hands. But they didn't. They progressed up the long dining-hall in a series of bounds or jumps. At the highest point of each jump a dish would be about fifteen feet up in the air; then it would come down and stop quite suddenly about three feet from the floor. When the dish contained anything like soup or stew the result was rather disastrous.

"I'm beginning to feel very inquisitive about these people," whispered Eustace to Edmund. "Do you think they're human at all? More like huge grasshoppers or giant frogs, I should say."

"It does look like it," said Edmund. "But don't put the idea of the grasshoppers into Lucy's head. She's not too keen on insects; especially big ones."

The meal would have been pleasanter if it had not been so exceedingly messy, and also if the conversation had not consisted entirely of agreements. The invisible people agreed about everything. Indeed most of their remarks were the sort it would not be easy to disagree with: "What I always say is, when a chap's hungry, he likes some victuals," or "Getting dark now; always does at night," or even "Ah, you've come over the water. Powerful wet stuff, ain't it?" And Lucy could not help looking at the dark yawning entrance to the foot of the staircase—she could see it from where she sat—and wondering what she would find when she went up those stairs next morning. But it was a good meal otherwise, with mushroom soup and boiled chickens and hot boiled ham and gooseberries, redcurrants, curds, cream, milk, and mead. The others liked the mead but Eustace was sorry afterward that he had drunk any.

When Lucy woke up next morning it was like waking up on the day of an examination or a day when you are going to the dentist. It was a lovely morning with bees buzzing in and out of her open window and the lawn outside looking very like somewhere in England. She got up and dressed and tried to talk and eat ordinarily at breakfast. Then, after being instructed by the Chief Voice about what she was to do upstairs, she bid good-bye to the others, said nothing, walked to the bottom of the stairs, and began going up them without once looking back.

It was quite light, that was one good thing. There was, indeed, a window straight ahead of her at the top of the first flight. As long as she was on that flight she could hear the *tick-tock-tick-tock* of a grandfather clock in the hall below. Then she came to the landing and had to turn to her left up the next flight; after that she couldn't hear the clock any more.

Now she had come to the top of the stairs. Lucy looked and saw a long, wide passage with a large window at the far end. Apparently the passage ran the whole length of the house. It was carved and paneled and carpeted and very many doors opened off it on each side. She stood still and couldn't hear the squeak of a mouse, or the buzzing of a fly, or the swaying of a curtain, or anything—except the beating of her own heart.

"The last doorway on the left," she said to herself. It did seem a bit hard that it should be the last. To reach it she would have to walk past room after room. And in any room there might be the magician—asleep, or awake, or invisible, or even dead. But it wouldn't do to think about that. She set out on her journey. The carpet was so thick that her feet made no noise.

"There's nothing whatever to be afraid of yet," Lucy told herself. And certainly it was a quiet, sunlit passage; perhaps a bit too quiet. It would have been nicer if there had not been strange signs painted in scarlet on the doors—twisty, complicated things which obviously had a meaning and it mightn't be a very nice meaning either. It would have been nicer still if there weren't those masks hanging on the wall. Not that they were exactly ugly—or not so very ugly—but the empty eye-holes did look queer, and if you let yourself you would soon start imagining that the masks were doing things as soon as your back was turned to them.

After about the sixth door she got her first real fright. For one second she felt almost certain that a wicked little bearded face had popped out of the wall and made a grimace at her. She forced herself to stop and look at it. And it was not a face at all. It was a little mirror just the size and shape of her own face, with hair on the top of it and a beard hanging down from it, so that when you looked in the mirror your own face fitted into the hair and beard and it looked as if they belonged to you. "I just caught my own reflection with the tail of my eye as I went past," said Lucy to herself. "That was all it was. It's quite harmless." But she didn't like the look of her own face with that hair and beard, and went on. (I don't know what the Bearded Glass was for because I am not a magician.)

Before she reached the last door on the left, Lucy was beginning to wonder whether the corri-

dor had grown longer since she began her journey and whether this was part of the magic of the house. But she got to it at last. And the door was open.

It was a large room with three big windows and it was lined from floor to ceiling with books; more books than Lucy had ever seen before, tiny little books, fat and dumpy books, and books bigger than any church Bible you have ever seen, all bound in leather and smelling old and learned and magical. But she knew from her instructions that she need not bother about any of these. For *the* Book, the Magic Book, was lying on a reading-desk in the very middle of the room. She saw she would have to read it standing (and anyway there were no chairs) and also that she would have to stand with her back to the door while she read it. So at once she turned to shut the door.

It wouldn't shut.

Some people may disagree with Lucy about this, but I think she was quite right. She said she wouldn't have minded if she could have shut the door, but that it was unpleasant to have to stand in a place like that with an open doorway right behind your back. I should have felt just the same. But there was nothing else to be done.

One thing that worried her a good deal was the size of the Book. The Chief Voice had not been able to give her any idea whereabouts in the Book the spell for making things visible came. He even seemed rather surprised at her asking. He expected her to begin at the beginning and go on till she came to it; obviously he had never thought that there was any other way of finding a place in a book. "But it might take me days and weeks!" said Lucy, looking at the huge volume, "and I feel already as if I'd been in this place for hours."

She went up to the desk and laid her hand on the book; her fingers tingled when she touched it as if it were full of electricity. She tried to open it but couldn't at first; this, however, was only because it was fastened by two leaden clasps, and when she had undone these it opened easily enough. And what a book it was!

It was written, not printed; written in a clear, even hand, with thick downstrokes and thin upstrokes, very large, easier than print, and so beautiful that Lucy stared at it for a whole minute and forgot about reading it. The paper was crisp and smooth and a nice smell came from it; and in the margins, and round the big colored capital letters at the beginning of each spell, there were pictures.

There was no title page or title; the spells began straight away, and at first there was nothing very important in them. They were cures for warts (by washing your hands in moonlight in a silver basin) and toothache and cramp, and a spell for taking a swarm of bees. The picture of the man

Cure for warts: wash in a silver basin by moonlight.

with toothache was so lifelike that it would have set your own teeth aching if you looked at it too long, and the golden bees which were dotted all round the fourth spell looked for a moment as if they were really flying.

Lucy could hardly tear herself away from that first page, but when she turned over, the next was just as interesting. "But I must get on," she told herself. And on she went for about thirty pages which, if she could have remembered them, would have taught her how to find buried treasure, how to remember things forgotten, how to forget things you wanted to forget, how to tell whether anyone was speaking the truth, how to call up (or prevent) wind, fog, snow, sleet or rain, how to produce enchanted sleeps and how to give a man an ass's head (as they did to poor Bottom). And the longer she read the more wonderful and more real the pictures became.

Then she came to a page which was such a blaze of pictures that one hardly noticed the writing. Hardly—but she *did* notice the first words. They were, *An infallible spell to make beautiful her that uttereth it beyond the lot of mortals.* Lucy peered at the pictures with her face close to the page, and though they had seemed crowded and muddlesome before, she found she could now see them quite clearly. The first was a picture of a girl standing at a reading-desk reading in a huge book. And the girl was dressed exactly like Lucy. In the next picture Lucy (for the girl in the picture was Lucy herself) was standing up with her mouth open and a rather terrible expression on her face, chanting or reciting something. In the third picture the beauty beyond the lot of mortals had come to her. It was strange, considering how small the pictures had looked at first, that the Lucy in the picture now seemed quite as big as the real Lucy; and they looked into each other's eyes and the real Lucy looked away after a few minutes because she was dazzled by the beauty of the other Lucy; though she could still see a sort of likeness to herself in that beautiful face. And now the pictures came crowding on her thick and fast. She saw herself throned on high at a great tournament in

Calormen and all the Kings of the world fought because of her beauty. After that it turned from tournaments to real wars, and all Narnia and Archenland, Telmar and Calormen, Galma and Terebinthia, were laid waste with the fury of the kings and dukes and great lords who fought for her favor. Then it changed and Lucy, still beautiful beyond the lot of mortals, was back in England. And Susan (who had always been the beauty of the family) came home from America. The Susan in the picture looked exactly like the real Susan only plainer and with a nasty expression. And Susan was jealous of the dazzling beauty of Lucy, but that didn't matter a bit because no one cared anything about Susan now.

"I *will* say the spell," said Lucy. "I don't care. I will." She said *I don't care* because she had a strong feeling that she mustn't.

But when she looked back at the opening words of the spell, there in the middle of the writing, where she felt quite sure there had been no picture before, she found the great face of a lion, of The Lion, Aslan himself, staring into hers. It was painted such a bright gold that it seemed to be coming toward her out of the page; and indeed she never was quite sure afterward that it hadn't really moved a little. At any rate she knew the expression on his face quite well. He was growling and you could see most of his teeth. She became horribly afraid and turned over the page at once.

A little later she came to a spell which would let you know what your friends thought about you. Now Lucy had wanted very badly to try the other spell, the one that made you beautiful beyond the lot of mortals. So she felt that to make up for not having said it, she really would say this one. And all in a hurry, for fear her mind would change, she said the words (nothing will induce me to tell you what they were). Then she waited for something to happen.

As nothing happened she began looking at the pictures. And all at once she saw the very last thing she expected—a picture of a third-class carriage in a train, with two schoolgirls sitting in it. She knew them at once. They were Marjorie Preston and Anne Featherstone. Only now it was much more than a picture. It was alive. She could see the telegraph posts flicking past outside the window. Then gradually (like when the radio is "coming on") she could hear what they were saying.

"Shall I see anything of you this term?" said Anne, "or are you still going to be all taken up with Lucy Pevensie."

"Don't know what you mean by *taken up*," said Marjorie.

"Oh yes, you do," said Anne. "You were crazy about her last term."

"No, I wasn't," said Marjorie. "I've got more

sense than that. Not a bad little kid in her way. But I was getting pretty tired of her before the end of term."

"Well, you jolly well won't have the chance any other term!" shouted Lucy. "Two-faced little beast." But the sound of her own voice at once reminded her that she was talking to a picture and that the real Marjorie was far away in another world.

"Well," said Lucy to herself, "I did think better of her than that. And I did all sorts of things for her last term, and I stuck to her when not many other girls would. And she knows it too. And to Anne Featherstone, of all people! I wonder are all my friends the same? There are lots of other pictures. No. I won't look at any more. I won't, I won't"—and with a great effort she turned over the page, but not before a large, angry tear had splashed on it.

On the next page she came to a spell "for the refreshment of the spirit." The pictures were fewer here but very beautiful. And what Lucy found herself reading was more like a story than a spell. It went on for three pages and before she had read to the bottom of the page she had forgotten that she was reading at all. She was living in the story as if it were real, and all the pictures were real too. When she had got to the third page and come to the end, she said, "That is the loveliest story I've ever read or ever shall read in my whole life. Oh, I wish I could have gone on reading it for ten years. At least I'll read it over again."

But here part of the magic of the Book came into play. You couldn't turn back. The right-hand pages, the ones ahead, could be turned; the left-hand pages could not.

"Oh, what a shame!" said Lucy. "I did so want to read it again. Well, at least I must remember it. Let's see . . . it was about . . . about . . . oh dear, it's all fading away again. And even this last page is going blank. This is a very queer book. How can I have forgotten? It was about a cup and a sword and a tree and a green hill, I know that much. But I can't remember and what *shall* I do?"

And she never could remember; and ever since that day what Lucy means by a good story is a story which reminds her of the forgotten story in the Magician's Book.

She turned on and found to her surprise a page with no pictures at all; but the first words were *A Spell to make hidden things visible*. She read it through to make sure of all the hard words and then said it out loud. And she knew at once that it was working because as she spoke the colors came into the capital letters at the top of the page and the pictures began appearing in the margins. It was like when you hold to the fire something written in Invisible Ink and the writing gradually shows up; only instead of the dingy color of lemon juice (which is the easiest Invisible Ink) this was all gold and blue and scarlet. They were odd pictures and contained many figures that Lucy did not much like the look of. And then she thought, "I suppose I've made everything visible, and not only the Thumpers. There might be lots of other invisible things hanging about a place like this. I'm not sure that I want to see them all."

At that moment she heard soft, heavy footfalls coming along the corridor behind her; and of course she remembered what she had been told about the Magician walking in his bare feet and making no more noise than a cat. It is always better to turn round than to have anything creeping up behind your back. Lucy did so.

Then her face lit up till, for a moment (but of course she didn't know it), she looked almost as beautiful as that other Lucy in the picture, and she ran forward with a little cry of delight and with her arms stretched out. For what stood in the doorway was Aslan himself, The Lion, the highest of all High Kings. And he was solid and real and warm and he let her kiss him and bury herself in his shining mane. And from the low, earthquake-like sound that came from inside him, Lucy even dared to think that he was purring.

"Oh, Aslan," said she, "it was kind of you to come."

"I have been here all the time," said he, "but you have just made me visible."

"Aslan!" said Lucy almost a little reproachfully. "Don't make fun of me. As if anything *I* could do would make *you* visible!"

"It did," said Aslan. "Do you think I wouldn't obey my own rules?"

After a little pause he spoke again.

"Child," he said, "I think you have been eavesdropping."

"Eavesdropping?"

"You listened to what your two schoolfellows were saying about you."

"Oh that? I never thought that was eavesdropping, Aslan. Wasn't it magic?"

"Spying on people by magic is the same as spying on them in any other way. And you have misjudged your friend. She is weak, but she loves you. She was afraid of the older girl and said what she does not mean."

"I don't think I'd ever be able to forget what I heard her say."

"No, you won't."

"Oh dear," said Lucy. "Have I spoiled everything? Do you mean we would have gone on being friends if it hadn't been for this—and been really great friends—all our lives perhaps—and now we never shall."

"Child," said Aslan, "did I not explain to you

once before that no one is ever told what *would have happened*?"

"Yes, Aslan, you did," said Lucy. "I'm sorry. But please—"

"Speak on, dear heart."

"Shall I ever be able to read that story again; the one I couldn't remember? Will you tell it to me, Aslan? Oh do, do, do."

"Indeed, yes, I will tell it to you for years and years. But now, come. We must meet the master of this house."

Eleven

THE DUFFLEPUDS
MADE HAPPY

LUCY FOLLOWED THE GREAT LION OUT
into the passage and at once she saw coming toward them an old man, barefoot, dressed in a red
robe. His white hair was crowned with a chaplet of
oak leaves, his beard fell to his girdle, and he supported himself with a curiously carved staff. When
he saw Aslan he bowed low and said,

"Welcome, Sir, to the least of your houses."

"Do you grow weary, Coriakin, of ruling such
foolish subjects as I have given you here?"

"No," said the Magician, "they are very stupid
but there is no real harm in them. I begin to grow
rather fond of the creatures. Sometimes, perhaps, I
am a little impatient, waiting for the day when
they can be governed by wisdom instead of this
rough magic."

"All in good time, Coriakin," said Aslan.

"Yes, all in very good time, Sir," was the answer. "Do you intend to show yourself to them?"

"Nay," said the Lion, with a little half-growl that meant (Lucy thought) the same as a laugh. "I should frighten them out of their senses. Many stars will grow old and come to take their rest in islands before your people are ripe for that. And today before sunset I must visit Trumpkin the Dwarf where he sits in the castle of Cair Paravel counting the days till his master Caspian comes home. I will tell him all your story, Lucy. Do not look so sad. We shall meet soon again."

"Please, Aslan," said Lucy, "what do you call *soon*?"

"I call all times soon," said Aslan; and instantly he was vanished away and Lucy was alone with the Magician.

"Gone!" said he, "and you and I quite crestfallen. It's always like that, you can't keep him; it's not as if he were a *tame* lion. And how did you enjoy my book?"

"Parts of it very much indeed," said Lucy. "Did you know I was there all the time?"

"Well, of course I knew when I let the Duffers make themselves invisible that you would be coming along presently to take the spell off. I wasn't quite sure of the exact day. And I wasn't especially on the watch this morning. You see they had made me invisible too and being invisible always makes me so sleepy. Heigh-ho—there I'm yawning again. Are you hungry?"

"Well, perhaps I am a little," said Lucy. "I've no idea what the time is."

"Come," said the Magician. "All times may be soon to Aslan; but in my home all hungry times are one o'clock."

He led her a little way down the passage and opened a door. Passing in, Lucy found herself in a pleasant room full of sunlight and flowers. The table was bare when they entered, but it was of course a magic table, and at a word from the old man the tablecloth, silver, plates, glasses and food appeared.

"I hope that is what you would like," said he. "I have tried to give you food more like the food of your own land than perhaps you have had lately."

"It's lovely," said Lucy, and so it was; an omelette, piping hot, cold lamb and green peas, a strawberry ice, lemon-squash to drink with the meal and a cup of chocolate to follow. But the magician himself drank only wine and ate only bread. There was nothing alarming about him, and Lucy and he were soon chatting away like old friends.

"When will the spell work?" asked Lucy. "Will the Duffers be visible again at once?"

"Oh yes, they're visible now. But they're probably all asleep still; they always take a rest in the middle of the day."

"And now that they're visible, are you going to

let them off being ugly? Will you make them as they were before?"

"Well, that's rather a delicate question," said the Magician. "You see, it's only *they* who think they were so nice to look at before. They say they've been uglified, but that isn't what I called it. Many people might say the change was for the better."

"Are they awfully conceited?"

"They are. Or at least the Chief Duffer is, and he's taught all the rest to be. They always believe every word he says."

"We'd noticed that," said Lucy.

"Yes—we'd get on better without him, in a way. Of course I could turn him into something else, or even put a spell on him which would make them not believe a word he said. But I don't like to do that. It's better for them to admire him than to admire nobody."

"Don't they admire *you*?" asked Lucy.

"Oh, not *me*," said the Magician. "They wouldn't admire *me*."

"What was it you uglified them for—I mean, what they call *uglified*?"

"Well, they wouldn't do what they were told. Their work is to mind the garden and raise food—not for me, as they imagine, but for themselves. They wouldn't do it at all if I didn't make them. And of course for a garden you want water. There is a beautiful spring about half a mile away up the hill. And from that spring there flows a stream which comes right past the garden. All I asked them to do was to take their water from the stream instead of trudging up to the spring with their buckets two or three times a day and tiring themselves out besides spilling half of it on the way back. But they wouldn't see it. In the end they refused point blank."

"Are they as stupid as all that?" asked Lucy.

The Magician sighed. "You wouldn't believe the troubles I've had with them. A few months ago they were all for washing up the plates and knives before dinner: they said it saved time afterward. I've caught them planting boiled potatoes to save cooking them when they were dug up. One day the cat got into the dairy and twenty of them were at work moving all the milk out; no one thought of moving the cat. But I see you've finished. Let's go and look at the Duffers now they can be looked at."

They went into another room which was full of polished instruments hard to understand—such as Astrolabes, Orreries, Chronoscopes, Poesimeters, Choriambuses and Theodolinds—and here, when they had come to the window, the Magician said, "There. There are your Duffers."

"I don't see anybody," said Lucy. "And what are those mushroom things?"

The things she pointed at were dotted all over

the level grass. They were certainly very like mushrooms, but far too big—the stalks about three feet high and the umbrellas about the same length from edge to edge. When she looked carefully she noticed too that the stalks joined the umbrellas not in the middle but at one side which gave an unbalanced look to them. And there was something—a sort of little bundle—lying on the grass at the foot of each stalk. In fact the longer she gazed at them the less like mushrooms they appeared. The umbrella part was not really round as she had thought at first. It was longer than it was broad, and it widened at one end. There were a great many of them, fifty or more.

The clock struck three.

Instantly a most extraordinary thing happened. Each of the "mushrooms" suddenly turned upside-down. The little bundles which had lain at the bottom of the stalks were heads and bodies. The stalks themselves were legs. But not two legs to each body. Each body had a single thick leg right under it (not to one side like the leg of a one-legged man) and at the end of it, a single enormous foot—a broad-toed foot with the toes curling up a little so that it looked rather like a small canoe. She saw in a moment why they had looked like mushrooms. They had been lying flat on their backs each with its single leg straight up in the air and its enormous foot spread out above it. She learned afterward that this was their ordinary way of resting; for the foot kept off both rain and sun and for a Monopod to lie under its own foot is almost as good as being in a tent.

"Oh, the funnies, the funnies," cried Lucy, bursting into laughter. "Did *you* make them like that?"

"Yes, yes. I made the Duffers into Monopods," said the Magician. He too was laughing till the tears ran down his cheeks. "But watch," he added.

It was worth watching. Of course these little one-footed men couldn't walk or run as we do. They got about by jumping, like fleas or frogs. And what jumps they made!—as if each big foot were a mass of springs. And with what a bounce they came down; that was what made the thumping noise which had so puzzled Lucy yesterday. For now they were jumping in all directions and calling out to one another, "Hey, lads! We're visible again."

"Visible we are," said one in a tasseled red cap who was obviously the Chief Monopod. "And what I say is, when chaps are visible, why, they can see one another."

"Ah, there it is, there it is, Chief," cried all the others. "There's the point. No one's got a clearer head than you. You couldn't have made it plainer."

"She caught the old man napping, that little girl did," said the Chief Monopod. "We've beaten him this time."

"Just what we were going to say ourselves," chimed the chorus. "You're going stronger than ever today, Chief. Keep it up, keep it up."

"But do they dare to talk about you like that?" said Lucy. "They seemed to be so afraid of you yesterday. Don't they know you might be listening?"

"That's one of the funny things about the Duffers," said the Magician. "One minute they talk as if I ran everything and overheard everything and was extremely dangerous. The next moment they think they can take me in by tricks that a baby would see through—bless them!"

"Will they have to be turned back into their proper shapes?" asked Lucy. "Oh, I do hope it wouldn't be unkind to leave them as they are. Do they really mind very much? They seem pretty happy. I say—look at that jump. What were they like before?"

"Common little dwarfs," said he. "Nothing like so nice as the sort you have in Narnia."

"It *would* be a pity to change them back," said Lucy. "They're so funny: and they're rather nice. Do you think it would make any difference if I told them that?"

"I'm sure it would—if you could get it into their heads."

"Will you come with me and try?"

"No, no. You'll get on far better without me."

"Thanks awfully for the lunch," said Lucy and turned quickly away. She ran down the stairs which she had come up so nervously that morning and cannoned into Edmund at the bottom. All the others were there with him waiting, and Lucy's conscience smote her when she saw their anxious faces and realized how long she had forgotten them.

"It's all right," she shouted. "Everything's all right. The Magician's a brick—and I've seen *Him*—Aslan."

After that she went from them like the wind and out into the garden. Here the earth was shaking with the jumps and the air ringing with the shouts of the Monopods. Both were redoubled when they caught sight of her.

"Here she comes, here she comes," they cried. "Three cheers for the little girl. Ah! She put it across the old gentleman properly, she did."

"And we're extremely regrettable," said the Chief Monopod, "that we can't give you the pleasure of seeing us as we were before we were uglified, for you wouldn't believe the difference, and that's the truth, for there's no denying we're mortal ugly now, so we won't deceive you."

"Eh, that we are, Chief, that we are," echoed the others, bouncing like so many toy balloons. "You've said it, you've said it."

"But I don't think you are at all," said Lucy, shouting to make herself heard. "I think you look very nice."

"Hear her, hear her," said the Monopods. "True for you, Missie. Very nice we look. You couldn't find a handsomer lot." They said this without any surprise and did not seem to notice that they had changed their minds.

"She's a-saying," remarked the Chief Monopod, "as how we looked very nice before we were ugli-fied."

"True for you, Chief, true for you," chanted the others. "That's what she says. We heard her our-selves."

"I did *not*," bawled Lucy. "I said you're very nice *now*."

"So she did, so she did," said the Chief Mono-pod, "said we were very nice then."

"Hear 'em both, hear 'em both," said the Monopods. "There's a pair for you. Always right. They couldn't have put it better."

"But we're saying just the opposite," said Lucy, stamping her foot with impatience.

"So you are, to be sure, so you are," said the Monopods. "Nothing like an opposite. Keep it up, both of you."

"You're enough to drive anyone mad," said Lucy, and gave it up. But the Monopods seemed perfectly contented, and she decided that on the whole the conversation had been a success.

And before everyone went to bed that evening something else happened which made them even more satisfied with their one-legged condition. Caspian and all the Narnians went back as soon as possible to the shore to give their news to Rhince and the others on board the *Dawn Treader*, who were by now very anxious. And, of course, the Monopods went with them, bouncing like footballs and agreeing with one another in loud voices till Eustace said, "I wish the Magician would make them inaudible instead of invisible." (He was soon sorry he had spoken because then he had to explain that an inaudible thing is something you can't hear, and though he took a lot of trouble he never felt sure that the Monopods had really understood, and what especially annoyed him was that they said in the end, "Eh, he can't put things the way our Chief does. But you'll learn, young man. Hark to *him*. He'll show you how to say things. There's a speaker for you!") When they reached the bay, Reepicheep had a brilliant idea. He had his little coracle lowered and paddled himself about in it till the Monopods were thoroughly interested. He then stood up in it and said, "Worthy and intelligent Monopods, you do not need boats. Each of you has a foot that will do instead. Just jump as lightly as you can on the water and see what happens."

The Chief Monopod hung back and warned the others that they'd find the water powerful wet, but one or two of the younger ones tried it almost at once; and then a few others followed their example, and at last the whole lot did the same. It worked perfectly. The huge single foot of a Monopod acted as a natural raft or boat, and when

Reepicheep had taught them how to cut rude paddles for themselves, they all paddled about the bay and round the *Dawn Treader*, looking for all the world like a fleet of little canoes with a fat dwarf standing up in the extreme stern of each. And they had races, and bottles of wine were lowered down to them from the ship as prizes, and the sailors stood leaning over the ship's sides and laughed till their own sides ached.

The Duffers were also very pleased with their new name of Monopods, which seemed to them a magnificent name though they never got it right. "That's what we are," they bellowed. "Moneypuds, Pomonods, Poddymons. Just what it was on the tips of our tongue to call ourselves." But they soon got it mixed up with their old name of Duffers and finally settled down to calling themselves the Dufflepuds; and that is what they will probably be called for centuries.

That evening all the Narnians dined upstairs with the Magician, and Lucy noticed how different the whole top floor looked now that she was no longer afraid of it. The mysterious signs on the doors were still mysterious but now looked as if they had kind and cheerful meanings, and even the bearded mirror now seemed funny rather than frightening. At dinner everyone had by magic what everyone liked best to eat and drink, and after dinner the Magician did a very useful and beautiful piece of magic. He laid two blank sheets of parchment on the table and asked Drinian to give him an exact account of their voyage up to date: and as Drinian spoke, everything he described came out on the parchment in fine clear lines till at last each sheet was a splendid map of the Eastern Ocean, showing Galma, Terebinthia, the Seven Isles, the Lone Islands, Dragon Island, Burnt Island, Deathwater, and the land of the Duffers itself, all exactly the right sizes and in the right positions. They were the first maps ever made of those seas and better than any that have been made since without magic. For on these, though the towns and mountains looked at first just as they would on an ordinary map, when the Magician lent them a magnifying glass you saw that they were perfect little pictures of the real things, so that you could see the very castle and slave market and streets in Narrowhaven, all very clear though very distant, like things seen through the wrong end of a telescope. The only drawback was that the coastline of most of the islands was incomplete, for the map showed only what Drinian had seen with his own eyes. When they were finished the Magician kept one himself and presented the other to Caspian: it still hangs in his Chamber of Instruments at Cair Paravel. But the Magician could tell them nothing about seas or lands further east. He did, however, tell them that about seven years before a Narnian ship had put in at his waters and that she had on board the Lords Revilian, Argoz, Mavramorn and Rhoop: so they judged that the golden man they had seen lying in Deathwater must be the Lord Restimar.

Next day, the Magician magically mended the stern of the *Dawn Treader* where it had been damaged by the Sea Serpent and loaded her with useful gifts. There was a most friendly parting, and when she sailed, two hours after noon, all the Dufflepuds paddled out with her to the harbor mouth, and cheered until she was out of sound of their cheering.

Twelve

THE DARK ISLAND

AFTER THIS ADVENTURE THEY SAILED on south and a little east for twelve days with a gentle wind, the skies being mostly clear and the air warm, and saw no bird or fish, except that once there were whales spouting a long way to starboard. Lucy and Reepicheep played a good deal of chess at this time. Then on the thirteenth day, Edmund, from the fighting-top, sighted what looked like a great dark mountain rising out of the sea on their port bow.

They altered course and made for this land, mostly by oar, for the wind would not serve them to sail northeast. When evening fell they were still a long way from it and rowed all night. Next morning the weather was fair but a flat calm. The dark mass lay ahead, much nearer and larger, but still very dim, so that some thought it was still a long way off and others thought they were running into a mist.

About nine that morning, very suddenly, it was

so close that they could see that it was not land at all, nor even, in an ordinary sense, a mist. It was a Darkness. It is rather hard to describe, but you will see what it was like if you imagine yourself looking into the mouth of a railway tunnel—a tunnel either so long or so twisty that you cannot see the light at the far end. And you know what it would be like. For a few feet you would see the rails and sleepers and gravel in broad daylight; then there would come a place where they were in twilight; and then, pretty suddenly, but of course without a sharp dividing line, they would vanish altogether into smooth, solid blackness. It was just so here. For a few feet in front of their bows they could see the swell of the bright greenish-blue water. Beyond that, they could see the water looking pale and gray as it would look late in the evening. But beyond that again, utter blackness as if they had come to the edge of moonless and starless night.

Caspian shouted to the boatswain to keep her back, and all except the rowers rushed forward and gazed from the bows. But there was nothing to be seen by gazing. Behind them was the sea and the sun, before them the Darkness.

"Do we go into this?" asked Caspian at length.

"Not by my advice," said Drinian.

"The Captain's right," said several sailors.

"I almost think he is," said Edmund.

Lucy and Eustace didn't speak but they felt

very glad inside at the turn things seemed to be taking. But all at once the clear voice of Reepicheep broke in upon the silence.

"And why not?" he said. "Will someone explain to me why not."

No one was anxious to explain, so Reepicheep continued:

"If I were addressing peasants or slaves," he said, "I might suppose that this suggestion proceeded from cowardice. But I hope it will never be told in Narnia that a company of noble and royal persons in the flower of their age turned tail because they were afraid of the dark."

"But what manner of use would it be plowing through that blackness?" asked Drinian.

"Use?" replied Reepicheep. "Use, Captain? If by use you mean filling our bellies or our purses, I confess it will be no use at all. So far as I know we did not set sail to look for things useful but to seek honor and adventure. And here is as great an adventure as ever I heard of, and here, if we turn back, no little impeachment of all our honors."

Several of the sailors said things under their breath that sounded like "Honor be blowed," but Caspian said:

"Oh, *bother* you, Reepicheep. I almost wish we'd left you at home. All right! If you put it that way, I suppose we shall have to go on. Unless Lucy would rather not?"

Lucy felt that she would very much rather not, but what she said out loud was, "I'm game."

"Your Majesty will at least order lights?" said Drinian.

"By all means," said Caspian. "See to it, Captain."

So the three lanterns, at the stern, and the prow and the masthead, were all lit, and Drinian ordered two torches amidships. Pale and feeble they looked in the sunshine. Then all the men except some who were left below at the oars were ordered on deck and fully armed and posted in their battle stations with swords drawn. Lucy and two archers were posted on the fighting-top with bows bent and arrows on the string. Rynelf was in the bows with his line ready to take soundings. Reepicheep, Edmund, Eustace and Caspian, glittering in mail, were with him. Drinian took the tiller.

"And now, in Aslan's name, forward!" cried Caspian. "A slow, steady stroke. And let every man be silent and keep his ears open for orders."

With a creak and a groan the *Dawn Treader* started to creep forward as the men began to row. Lucy, up in the fighting-top, had a wonderful view of the exact moment at which they entered the darkness. The bows had already disappeared before the sunlight had left the stern. She saw it go. At one minute the gilded stern, the blue sea, and the sky, were all in broad daylight: next minute

the sea and sky had vanished, the stern lantern—
which had been hardly noticeable before—was the
only thing to show where the ship ended. In front
of the lantern she could see the black shape of
Drinian crouching at the tiller. Down below her
the two torches made visible two small patches of
deck and gleamed on swords and helmets, and forward there was another island of light on the forecastle. Apart from that, the fighting-top, lit by the
masthead light which was only just above her,
seemed to be a little lighted world of its own floating in lonely darkness. And the lights themselves,
as always happens with lights when you have to
have them at the wrong time of day, looked lurid
and unnatural. She also noticed that she was very
cold.

How long this voyage into the darkness lasted,
nobody knew. Except for the creak of the rowlocks
and the splash of the oars there was nothing to
show that they were moving at all. Edmund, peering from the bows, could see nothing except the
reflection of the lantern in the water before him. It
looked a greasy sort of reflection, and the ripple
made by their advancing prow appeared to be
heavy, small, and lifeless. As time went on everyone except the rowers began to shiver with cold.

Suddenly, from somewhere—no one's sense of
direction was very clear by now—there came a
cry, either of some inhuman voice or else a voice of

one in such extremity of terror that he had almost lost his humanity.

Caspian was still trying to speak—his mouth was too dry—when the shrill voice of Reepicheep, which sounded louder than usual in that silence, was heard.

"Who calls?" it piped. "If you are a foe we do not fear you, and if you are a friend your enemies shall be taught the fear of us."

"Mercy!" cried the voice. "Mercy! Even if you are only one more dream, have mercy. Take me on board. Take me, even if you strike me dead. But in the name of all mercies do not fade away and leave me in this horrible land."

"Where are you?" shouted Caspian. "Come aboard and welcome."

There came another cry, whether of joy or terror, and then they knew that someone was swimming toward them.

"Stand by to heave him up, men," said Caspian.

"Aye, aye, your Majesty," said the sailors. Several crowded to the port bulwark with ropes and one, leaning far out over the side, held the torch. A wild, white face appeared in the blackness of the water, and then, after some scrambling and pulling, a dozen friendly hands had heaved the stranger on board.

Edmund thought he had never seen a wilder-looking man. Though he did not otherwise look very old, his hair was an untidy mop of white, his face was thin and drawn, and, for clothing, only a few wet rags hung about him. But what one mainly noticed were his eyes, which were so widely opened that he seemed to have no eyelids at all, and stared as if in an agony of pure fear. The moment his feet reached the deck he said:

"Fly! Fly! About with your ship and fly! Row, row, row for your lives away from this accursed shore."

"Compose yourself," said Reepicheep, "and tell us what the danger is. We are not used to flying."

The stranger started horribly at the voice of the Mouse, which he had not noticed before.

"Nevertheless you will fly from here," he gasped. "This is the Island where Dreams come true."

"That's the island I've been looking for this long time," said one of the sailors. "I reckon I'd find I was married to Nancy if we landed here."

"And I'd find Tom alive again," said another.

"Fools!" said the man, stamping his foot with rage. "That is the sort of talk that brought me here, and I'd better have been drowned or never born. Do you hear what I say? This is where dreams—dreams, do you understand—come to life, come real. Not daydreams: dreams."

There was about half a minute's silence and then, with a great clatter of armor, the whole crew were tumbling down the main hatch as quick as they could and flinging themselves on the oars to row as they had never rowed before; and Drinian was swinging round the tiller, and the boatswain was giving out the quickest stroke that had ever been heard at sea. For it had taken everyone just that half-minute to remember certain dreams they had had—dreams that make you afraid of going to sleep again—and to realize what it would mean to land on a country where dreams come true.

Only Reepicheep remained unmoved.

"Your Majesty, your Majesty," he said, "are you going to tolerate this mutiny, this poltroonery? This is a panic, this is a rout."

"Row, row," bellowed Caspian. "Pull for all our lives. Is her head right, Drinian? You can say what you like, Reepicheep. There are some things no man can face."

"It is, then, my good fortune not to be a man," replied Reepicheep with a very stiff bow.

Lucy from up aloft had heard it all. In an instant that one of her own dreams which she had tried hardest to forget came back to her as vividly as if she had only just woken from it. So *that* was what was behind them, on the island, in the darkness! For a second she wanted to go down to the deck and be with Edmund and Caspian. But what was the use? If dreams began coming true, Edmund and Caspian themselves might turn into something horrible just as she reached them. She gripped the rail of the fighting-top and tried to steady herself. They were rowing back to the light as hard as they could: it would be all right in a few seconds. But oh, if only it could be all right now!

Though the rowing made a good deal of noise it did not quite conceal the total silence which surrounded the ship. Everyone knew it would be better not to listen, not to strain his ears for any sound from the darkness. But no one could help listening. And soon everyone was hearing things. Each one heard something different.

"Do you hear a noise like . . . like a huge pair of scissors opening and shutting . . . over there?" Eustace asked Rynelf.

"Hush!" said Rynelf. "I can hear *them* crawling up the sides of the ship."

"*It's* just going to settle on the mast," said Caspian.

"Ugh!" said a sailor. "There are the gongs beginning. I knew they would."

Caspian, trying not to look at anything (especially not to keep looking behind him), went aft to Drinian.

"Drinian," he said in a very low voice. "How long did we take rowing in?—I mean rowing to where we picked up the stranger."

"Five minutes, perhaps," whispered Drinian. "Why?"

"Because we've been more than that already trying to get out."

Drinian's hand shook on the tiller and a line of cold sweat ran down his face. The same idea was occurring to everyone on board. "We shall never get out, never get out," moaned the rowers. "He's steering us wrong. We're going round and round in circles. We shall never get out." The stranger, who had been lying in a huddled heap on the deck, sat up and burst out into a horrible screaming laugh.

"Never get out!" he yelled. "That's it. Of course. We shall never get out. What a fool I was to have thought they would let me go as easily as that. No, no, we shall never get out."

Lucy leant her head on the edge of the fighting-top and whispered, "Aslan, Aslan, if ever you loved us at all, send us help now." The darkness did not grow any less, but she began to feel a little—a very, very little—better. "After all, nothing has really happened to us yet," she thought.

"Look!" cried Rynelf's voice hoarsely from the bows. There was a tiny speck of light ahead, and while they watched a broad beam of light fell from it upon the ship. It did not alter the surrounding darkness, but the whole ship was lit up as if by searchlight. Caspian blinked, stared round, saw the faces of his companions all with wild, fixed expressions. Everyone was staring in the same direction: behind everyone lay his black, sharply edged shadow.

Lucy looked along the beam and presently saw something in it. At first it looked like a cross, then it looked like an aeroplane, then it looked like a kite, and at last with a whirring of wings it was right overhead and was an albatross. It circled three times round the mast and then perched for an instant on the crest of the gilded dragon at the prow. It called out in a strong sweet voice what seemed to be words though no one understood them. After that it spread its wings, rose, and began to fly slowly ahead, bearing a little to starboard. Drinian steered after it not doubting that it offered good guidance. But no one except Lucy knew that as it circled the mast it had whispered to her, "Courage, dear heart," and the voice, she felt sure, was Aslan's, and with the voice a delicious smell breathed in her face.

In a few moments the darkness turned into a grayness ahead, and then, almost before they dared to begin hoping, they had shot out into the sunlight and were in the warm, blue world again. And all at once everybody realized that there was nothing to be afraid of and never had been. They blinked their eyes and looked about them. The brightness of the ship herself astonished them: they had half expected to find that the darkness would cling to the white and the green and the gold in the form of some grime or scum. And then first one, and then another, began laughing.

"I reckon we've made pretty good fools of ourselves," said Rynelf.

Lucy lost no time in coming down to the deck, where she found the others all gathered round the newcomer. For a long time he was too happy to speak, and could only gaze at the sea and the sun and feel the bulwarks and the ropes, as if to make sure he was really awake, while tears rolled down his cheeks.

"Thank you," he said at last. "You have saved me from . . . but I won't talk of that. And now let me know who you are. I am a Telmarine of Narnia, and when I was worth anything men called me the Lord Rhoop."

"And I," said Caspian, "am Caspian, King of Narnia, and I sail to find you and your companions who were my father's friends."

Lord Rhoop fell on his knees and kissed the King's hand. "Sire," he said, "you are the man in all the world I most wished to see. Grant me a boon."

"What is it?" asked Caspian.

"Never to bring me back there," he said. He pointed astern. They all looked. But they saw only bright blue sea and bright blue sky. The Dark Island and the darkness had vanished for ever.

"Why!" cried Lord Rhoop. "You have destroyed it!"

"I don't think it was us," said Lucy.

"Sire," said Drinian, "this wind is fair for the southeast. Shall I have our poor fellows up and set sail? And after that, every man who can be spared, to his hammock."

"Yes," said Caspian, "and let there be grog all round. Heigh-ho, I feel I could sleep the clock round myself."

So all afternoon with great joy they sailed southeast with a fair wind. But nobody noticed when the albatross had disappeared.

Thirteen

THE THREE SLEEPERS

THE WIND NEVER FAILED BUT IT GREW gentler every day till at length the waves were little more than ripples, and the ship glided on hour after hour almost as if they were sailing on a lake. And every night they saw that there rose in the east new constellations which no one had ever seen in Narnia and perhaps, as Lucy thought with a mixture of joy and fear, no living eye had seen at all. Those new stars were big and bright and the nights were warm. Most of them slept on deck and talked far into the night or hung over the ship's side watching the luminous dance of the foam thrown up by their bows.

On an evening of startling beauty, when the sunset behind them was so crimson and purple and widely spread that the very sky itself seemed to have grown larger, they came in sight of land on their starboard bow. It came slowly nearer and the light behind them made it look as if the capes and headlands of this new country were all on fire. But presently they were sailing along its coast and its western cape now rose up astern of them, black against the red sky and sharp as if it was cut out of cardboard, and then they could see better what this country was like. It had no mountains but many gentle hills with slopes like pillows. An attractive smell came from it—what Lucy called "a dim, purple kind of smell," which Edmund said (and Rhince thought) was rot, but Caspian said, "I know what you mean."

They sailed on a good way, past point after point, hoping to find a nice deep harbor, but had to content themselves in the end with a wide and shallow bay. Though it had seemed calm out at sea there was of course surf breaking on the sand and they could not bring the *Dawn Treader* as far in as they would have liked. They dropped anchor a good way from the beach and had a wet and tumbling landing in the boat. The Lord Rhoop remained on board the *Dawn Treader*. He wished to see no more islands. All the time that they remained in this country the sound of the long breakers was in their ears.

Two men were left to guard the boat and Caspian led the others inland, but not far because it was too late for exploring and the light would soon go. But there was no need to go far to find an adventure. The level valley which lay at the head of the bay showed no road or track or other sign of habitation. Underfoot was fine springy turf dotted here and there with a low bushy growth which Edmund and Lucy took for heather. Eustace, who was really rather good at botany, said it wasn't, and he was probably right; but it was something of very much the same kind.

When they had gone less than a bowshot from the shore, Drinian said, "Look! What's that?" and everyone stopped.

"Are they great trees?" said Caspian.

"Towers, I think," said Eustace.

"It might be giants," said Edmund in a lower voice.

"The way to find out is to go right in among them," said Reepicheep, drawing his sword and pattering off ahead of everyone else.

"I think it's a ruin," said Lucy when they had got a good deal nearer, and her guess was the best so far. What they now saw was a wide oblong space flagged with smooth stones and surrounded by gray pillars but unroofed. And from end to end of it ran a long table laid with a rich crimson cloth that came down nearly to the pavement. At either side of it were many chairs of stone richly carved and with silken cushions upon the seats. But on the table itself there was set out such a banquet as had never been seen, not even when Peter the High King kept his court at Cair Paravel. There were turkeys and geese and peacocks, there were boars' heads and sides of venison, there were pies shaped like ships under full sail or like dragons and elephants, there were ice puddings and bright lobsters and gleaming salmon, there were nuts and grapes, pineapples and peaches, pomegranates and melons and tomatoes. There were flagons of gold and silver and curiously-wrought glass; and the smell of the fruit and the wine blew toward them like a promise of all happiness.

"I *say*!" said Lucy.

They came nearer and nearer, all very quietly.

"But where are the guests?" asked Eustace.

"We can provide that, Sir," said Rhince.

"Look!" said Edmund sharply. They were actually within the pillars now and standing on the pavement. Everyone looked where Edmund had pointed. The chairs were not all empty. At the head of the table and in the two places beside it there was something—or possibly three somethings.

"What are *those*?" asked Lucy in a whisper. "It looks like three beavers sitting on the table."

"Or a huge bird's nest," said Edmund.

"It looks more like a haystack to me," said Caspian.

Reepicheep ran forward, jumped on a chair and thence on to the table, and ran along it, threading his way as nimbly as a dancer between jeweled cups and pyramids of fruit and ivory salt-cellars.

He ran right up to the mysterious gray mass at the end: peered, touched, and then called out:

"These will not fight, I think."

Everyone now came close and saw that what sat in those three chairs was three men, though hard to recognize as men till you looked closely. Their hair, which was gray, had grown over their eyes till it almost concealed their faces, and their beards had grown over the table, climbing round and entwining plates and goblets as brambles entwine a fence, until, all mixed in one great mat of hair, they flowed over the edge and down to the floor. And from their heads the hair hung over the backs of their chairs so that they were wholly hidden. In fact the three men were nearly all hair.

"Dead?" said Caspian.

"I think not, Sire," said Reepicheep, lifting one of their hands out of its tangle of hair in his two paws. "This one is warm and his pulse beats."

"This one, too, and this," said Drinian.

"Why, they're only asleep," said Eustace.

"It's been a long sleep, though," said Edmund, "to let their hair grow like this."

"It must be an enchanted sleep," said Lucy. "I felt the moment we landed on this island that it was full of magic. Oh! do you think we have perhaps come here to break it?"

"We can try," said Caspian, and began shaking the nearest of the three sleepers. For a moment everyone thought he was going to be successful, for the man breathed hard and muttered, "I'll go eastward no more. Out oars for Narnia." But he sank back almost at once into a yet deeper sleep than before: that is, his heavy head sagged a few inches lower toward the table and all efforts to rouse him again were useless. With the second it was much the same. "Weren't born to live like animals. Get to the east while you've a chance—lands behind the sun," and sank down. And the third only said, "Mustard, please," and slept hard.

"*Out oars for Narnia*, eh?" said Drinian.

"Yes," said Caspian, "you are right, Drinian. I think our quest is at an end. Let's look at their rings. Yes, these are their devices. This is the Lord Revilian. This is the Lord Argoz: and this, the Lord Mavramorn."

"But we can't wake them," said Lucy. "What are we to do?"

"Begging your Majesties' pardons all," said Rhince, "but why not fall to while you're discussing it? We don't see a dinner like this every day."

"Not for your life!" said Caspian.

"That's right, that's right," said several of the sailors. "Too much magic about here. The sooner we're back on board the better."

"Depend upon it," said Reepicheep, "it was from eating this food that these three lords came by a seven years' sleep."

"I wouldn't touch it to save my life," said Drinian.

"The light's going uncommon quick," said Rynelf.

"Back to ship, back to ship," muttered the men.

"I really think," said Edmund, "they're right. We can decide what to do with the three sleepers tomorrow. We daren't eat the food and there's no point in staying here for the night. The whole place smells of magic—and danger."

"I am entirely of King Edmund's opinion," said Reepicheep, "as far as concerns the ship's company in general. But I myself will sit at this table till sunrise."

"Why on earth?" said Eustace.

"Because," said the Mouse, "this is a very great adventure, and no danger seems to me so great as that of knowing when I get back to Narnia that I left a mystery behind me through fear."

"I'll stay with you, Reep," said Edmund.

"And I too," said Caspian.

"And me," said Lucy. And then Eustace volunteered also. This was very brave of him because never having read of such things or even heard of them till he joined the *Dawn Treader* made it worse for him than for the others.

"I beseech your Majesty—" began Drinian.

"No, my Lord," said Caspian. "Your place is with the ship, and you have had a day's work while we five have idled." There was a lot of argument about this but in the end Caspian had his way. As the crew marched off to the shore in the gathering dusk none of the five watchers, except perhaps Reepicheep, could avoid a cold feeling in the stomach.

They took some time choosing their seats at the perilous table. Probably everyone had the same reason but no one said it out loud. For it was really a rather nasty choice. One could hardly bear to sit all night next to those three terrible hairy objects which, if not dead, were certainly not alive in the ordinary sense. On the other hand, to sit at the far end, so that you would see them less and less as the night grew darker, and wouldn't know if they were moving, and perhaps wouldn't see them at all by about two o'clock—no, it was not to be thought of. So they sauntered round and round the table saying, "What about here?" and "Or perhaps a bit further on," or, "Why not on this side?" till at last they settled down somewhere about the middle but nearer to the sleepers than to the other end. It was about ten by now and almost dark. Those strange new constellations burned in the east. Lucy would have liked it better if they had been the Leopard and the Ship and other old friends of the Narnian sky.

They wrapped themselves in their sea cloaks and sat still and waited. At first there was some attempt at talk but it didn't come to much. And they sat and sat. And all the time they heard the waves breaking on the beach.

After hours that seemed like ages there came a moment when they all knew they had been dozing a moment before but were all suddenly wide awake. The stars were all in quite different positions from those they had last noticed. The sky was very black except for the faintest possible grayness in the east. They were cold, though thirsty, and stiff. And none of them spoke because now at last something was happening.

Before them, beyond the pillars, there was the

slope of a low hill. And now a door opened in the hillside, and light appeared in the doorway, and a figure came out, and the door shut behind it. The figure carried a light, and this light was really all that they could see distinctly. It came slowly nearer and nearer till at last it stood right at the table opposite to them. Now they could see that it was a tall girl, dressed in a single long garment of clear blue which left her arms bare. She was bareheaded and her yellow hair hung down her back. And when they looked at her they thought they had never before known what beauty meant.

The light which she had been carrying was a tall candle in a silver candlestick which she now set upon the table. If there had been any wind off the sea earlier in the night it must have died down by now, for the flame of the candle burned as straight and still as if it were in a room with the windows shut and the curtains drawn. Gold and silver on the table shone in its light.

Lucy now noticed something lying lengthwise on the table which had escaped her attention before. It was a knife of stone, sharp as steel, a cruel-looking, ancient-looking thing.

No one had yet spoken a word. Then—Reepicheep first, and Caspian next—they all rose to their feet, because they felt that she was a great lady.

"Travelers who have come from far to Aslan's table," said the girl. "Why do you not eat and drink?"

"Madam," said Caspian, "we feared the food because we thought it had cast our friends into an enchanted sleep."

"They have never tasted it," she said.

"Please," said Lucy, "what happened to them?"

"Seven years ago," said the girl, "they came here in a ship whose sails were rags and her timbers ready to fall apart. There were a few others with them, sailors, and when they came to this table one said, 'Here is the good place. Let us set sail and reef sail and row no longer but sit down and end our days in peace!' And the second said, 'No, let us re-embark and sail for Narnia and the west; it may be that Miraz is dead.' But the third, who was a very masterful man, leaped up and said, 'No, by heaven. We are men and Telmarines, not brutes. What should we do but seek adventure after adventure? We have not long to live in any event. Let us spend what is left in seeking the unpeopled world behind the sunrise.' And as they quarreled he caught up the Knife of Stone which lies there on the table and would have fought with his comrades. But it is a thing not right for him to touch. And as his fingers closed upon the hilt, deep sleep fell upon all the three. And till the enchantment is undone they will never wake."

"What is this Knife of Stone?" asked Eustace.

"Do none of you know it?" said the girl.

"I—I think," said Lucy, "I've seen something like it before. It was a knife like it that the White Witch used when she killed Aslan at the Stone Table long ago."

"It was the same," said the girl, "and it was brought here to be kept in honor while the world lasts."

Edmund, who had been looking more and more uncomfortable for the last few minutes, now spoke.

"Look here," he said, "I hope I'm not a coward—about eating this food, I mean—and I'm sure I don't mean to be rude. But we have had a lot of queer adventures on this voyage of ours and things aren't always what they seem. When I look in your face I can't help believing all you say: but then that's just what might happen with a witch too. How are we to know you're a friend?"

"You can't know," said the girl. "You can only believe—or not."

After a moment's pause Reepicheep's small voice was heard.

"Sire," he said to Caspian, "of your courtesy fill my cup with wine from that flagon: it is too big for me to lift. I will drink to the lady."

Caspian obeyed and the Mouse, standing on the table, held up a golden cup between its tiny paws and said, "Lady, I pledge you." Then it fell to on cold peacock, and in a short while everyone else followed his example. All were very hungry and the meal, if not quite what you wanted for a very early breakfast, was excellent as a very late supper.

"Why is it called Aslan's table?" asked Lucy presently.

"It is set here by his bidding," said the girl, "for those who come so far. Some call this island the World's End, for though you can sail further, this is the beginning of the end."

"But how does the food *keep*?" asked the practical Eustace.

"It is eaten, and renewed every day," said the girl. "This you will see."

"And what are we to do about the Sleepers?" asked Caspian. "In the world from which my friends come" (here he nodded at Eustace and the Pevensies) "they have a story of a prince or a king coming to a castle where all the people lay in an enchanted sleep. In that story he could not dissolve the enchantment until he had kissed the Princess."

"But here," said the girl, "it is different. Here he cannot kiss the Princess till he has dissolved the enchantment."

"Then," said Caspian, "in the name of Aslan, show me how to set about that work at once."

"My father will teach you that," said the girl.

"Your father!" said everyone. "Who is he? And where?"

"Look," said the girl, turning round and pointing at the door in the hillside. They could see it more easily now, for while they had been talking the stars had grown fainter and great gaps of white light were appearing in the grayness of the eastern sky.

Fourteen

THE BEGINNING OF
THE END OF THE WORLD

SLOWLY THE DOOR OPENED AGAIN AND out there came a figure as tall and straight as the girl's but not so slender. It carried no light but light seemed to come from it. As it came nearer, Lucy saw that it was like an old man. His silver beard came down to his bare feet in front and his silver hair hung down to his heels behind and his robe appeared to be made from the fleece of silver sheep. He looked so mild and grave that once more all the travelers rose to their feet and stood in silence.

But the old man came on without speaking to the travelers and stood on the other side of the table opposite to his daughter. Then both of them held up their arms before them and turned to face the east. In that position they began to sing. I wish I could write down the song, but no one who was present could remember it. Lucy said afterward that it was high, almost shrill, but very beautiful, "A cold kind of song, an early morning kind of song." And as they sang, the gray clouds lifted from the eastern sky and the white patches grew bigger and bigger till it was all white, and the sea began to shine like silver. And long afterward (but those two sang all the time) the east began to turn red and at last, unclouded, the sun came up out of the sea and its long level ray shot down the length of the table on the gold and silver and on the Stone Knife.

Once or twice before, the Narnians had wondered whether the sun at its rising did not look bigger in these seas than it had looked at home. This time they were certain. There was no mistaking it. And the brightness of its ray on the dew and on the table was far beyond any morning brightness they had ever seen. And as Edmund said afterward, "Though lots of things happened on that trip which *sound* more exciting, that moment was really the most exciting." For now they knew that they had truly come to the beginning of the End of the World.

Then something seemed to be flying at them out of the very center of the rising sun: but of course one couldn't look steadily in that direction to make sure. But presently the air became full of voices—voices which took up the same song that the Lady and her Father were singing, but in far wilder tones and in a language which no one knew. And soon after that the owners of these voices could be seen. They were birds, large and white, and they came by hundreds and thousands and alighted on everything; on the grass, and the pavement, on the table, on your shoulders, your hands, and your head, till it looked as if heavy snow had fallen. For, like snow, they not only made everything white but blurred and blunted all shapes. But Lucy, looking out from between the wings of the birds that covered her, saw one bird fly to the Old Man with something in its beak that looked like a little fruit, unless it was a little live coal, which it might have been, for it was too bright to look at. And the bird laid it in the Old Man's mouth.

Then the birds stopped their singing and appeared to be very busy about the table. When they rose from it again everything on the table that could be eaten or drunk had disappeared. These birds rose from their meal in their thousands and hundreds and carried away all the things that could not be eaten or drunk, such as bones, rinds, and shells, and took their flight back to the rising sun. But now, because they were not singing, the whir of their wings seemed to set the whole air a-tremble. And there was the table pecked clean and empty, and the three old Lords of Narnia still fast asleep.

Now at last the Old Man turned to the travelers and bade them welcome.

"Sir," said Caspian, "will you tell us how to undo the enchantment which holds these three Narnian Lords asleep."

"I will gladly tell you that, my son," said the Old Man. "To break this enchantment you must sail to the World's End, or as near as you can come to it, and you must come back having left at least one of your company behind."

"And what must happen to that one?" asked Reepicheep.

"He must go on into the utter east and never return into the world."

"That is my heart's desire," said Reepicheep.

"And are we near the World's End now, Sir?" asked Caspian. "Have you any knowledge of the seas and lands further east than this?"

"I saw them long ago," said the Old Man, "but it was from a great height. I cannot tell you such things as sailors need to know."

"Do you mean you were flying in the air?" Eustace blurted out.

"I was a long way above the air, my son," replied the Old Man. "I am Ramandu. But I see that you stare at one another and have not heard this name. And no wonder, for the days when I was a star had ceased long before any of you knew this world, and all the constellations have changed."

"Golly," said Edmund under his breath. "He's a *retired* star."

"Aren't you a star any longer?" asked Lucy.

"I am a star at rest, my daughter," answered Ramandu. "When I set for the last time, decrepit and old beyond all that you can reckon, I was carried to this island. I am not so old now as I was then. Every morning a bird brings me a fire-berry from the valleys in the Sun, and each fire-berry takes away a little of my age. And when I have become as young as the child that was born yesterday, then I shall take my rising again (for we are at earth's eastern rim) and once more tread the great dance."

"In our world," said Eustace, "a star is a huge ball of flaming gas."

"Even in your world, my son, that is not what a star is but only what it is made of. And in this world you have already met a star: for I think you have been with Coriakin."

"Is he a retired star, too?" said Lucy.

"Well, not quite the same," said Ramandu. "It was not quite as a rest that he was set to govern the Duffers. You might call it a punishment. He might have shone for thousands of years more in the southern winter sky if all had gone well."

"What did he do, Sir?" asked Caspian.

"My son," said Ramandu, "it is not for you, a son of Adam, to know what faults a star can commit. But come, we waste time in such talk. Are you yet resolved? Will you sail further east and come again, leaving one to return no more, and so break the enchantment? Or will you sail westward?"

"Surely, Sire," said Reepicheep, "there is no question about that? It is very plainly part of our quest to rescue these three lords from enchantment."

"I think the same, Reepicheep," replied Caspian. "And even if it were not so, it would break my heart not to go as near the World's End as the

Dawn Treader will take us. But I am thinking of the crew. They signed on to seek the seven lords, not to reach the rim of the Earth. If we sail east from here we sail to find the edge, the utter east. And no one knows how far it is. They're brave fellows, but I see signs that some of them are weary of the voyage and long to have our prow pointing to Narnia again. I don't think I should take them further without their knowledge and consent. And then there's the poor Lord Rhoop. He's a broken man."

"My son," said the star, "it would be no use, even though you wished it, to sail for the World's End with men unwilling or men deceived. That is not how great unenchantments are achieved. They must know where they go and why. But who is this broken man you speak of?"

Caspian told Ramandu the story of Rhoop.

"I can give him what he needs most," said Ramandu. "In this island there is sleep without stint or measure, and sleep in which no faintest footfall of a dream was ever heard. Let him sit beside these other three and drink oblivion till your return."

"Oh, do let's do that, Caspian," said Lucy. "I'm sure it's just what he would love."

At that moment they were interrupted by the sound of many feet and voices: Drinian and the rest of the ship's company were approaching. They halted in surprise when they saw Ramandu and his daughter; and then, because these were obviously great people, every man uncovered his head. Some sailors eyed the empty dishes and flagons on the table with eyes filled with regret.

"My lord," said the King to Drinian, "pray send two men back to the *Dawn Treader* with a message to the Lord Rhoop. Tell him that the last of his old shipmates are here asleep—a sleep without dreams—and that he can share it."

When this had been done, Caspian told the rest to sit down and laid the whole situation before them. When he had finished there was a long silence and some whispering until presently the Master Bowman got to his feet, and said:

"What some of us have been wanting to ask for a long time, your Majesty, is how we're ever to get home when we do turn, whether we turn here or somewhere else. It's been west and northwest winds all the way, barring an occasional calm. And if that doesn't change, I'd like to know what hopes we have of seeing Narnia again. There's not much chance of supplies lasting while we *row* all that way."

"That's landsman's talk," said Drinian. "There's always a prevailing west wind in these seas all through the late summer, and it always changes after the New Year. We'll have plenty of wind for sailing westward; more than we shall like from all accounts."

"That's true, Master," said an old sailor who was a Galmian by birth. "You get some ugly weather rolling up from the east in January and February. And by your leave, Sire, if I was in command of this ship, I'd say to winter here and begin the voyage home in March."

"What'd you eat while you were wintering here?" asked Eustace.

"This table," said Ramandu, "will be filled with a king's feast every day at sunset."

"Now you're talking!" said several sailors.

"Your Majesties and gentlemen and ladies all," said Rynelf, "there's just one thing I want to say. There's not one of us chaps as was pressed on this journey. We're volunteers. And there's some here that are looking very hard at that table and thinking about king's feasts who were talking very loud about adventures on the day we sailed from Cair Paravel, and swearing they wouldn't come home till we'd found the end of the world. And there were some standing on the quay who would have given all they had to come with us. It was thought a finer thing then to have a cabin-boy's berth on the *Dawn Treader* than to wear a knight's belt. I don't know if you get the hang of what I'm saying. But what I mean is that I think chaps who set out like us will look as silly as—as those Dufflepuds—if we come home and say we got to the beginning of the world's end and hadn't the heart to go further."

Some of the sailors cheered at this but some said that that was all very well.

"This isn't going to be much fun," whispered Edmund to Caspian. "What are we to do if half those fellows hang back?"

"Wait," Caspian whispered back. "I've still a card to play."

"Aren't you going to say anything, Reep?" whispered Lucy.

"No. Why should your Majesty expect it?" answered Reepicheep in a voice that most people heard. "My own plans are made. While I can, I sail east in the *Dawn Treader*. When she fails me, I paddle east in my coracle. When she sinks, I shall swim east with my four paws. And when I can swim no longer, if I have not reached Aslan's country, or shot over the edge of the world in some vast cataract, I shall sink with my nose to the sunrise and Peepiceek will be head of the talking mice in Narnia."

"Hear, hear," said a sailor. "I'll say the same, barring the bit about the coracle, which wouldn't bear me." He added in a lower voice, "I'm not going to be outdone by a mouse."

At this point Caspian jumped to his feet. "Friends," he said, "I think you have not quite understood our purpose. You talk as if we had come to you with our hat in our hand, begging for shipmates. It isn't like that at all. We and our royal

brother and sister and their kinsman and Sir
Reepicheep, the good knight, and the Lord Drinian
have an errand to the world's edge. It is our pleasure to choose from among such of you as are
willing those whom we deem worthy of so high an
enterprise. We have not said that any can come for
the asking. That is why we shall now command
the Lord Drinian and Master Rhince to consider
carefully what men among you are the hardest in
battle, the most skilled seamen, the purest in
blood, the most loyal to our person, and the clean-
est of life and manners; and to give their names to
us in a schedule." He paused and went on in a
quicker voice, "Aslan's mane!" he exclaimed. "Do
you think that the privilege of seeing the last
things is to be bought for a song? Why, every man
that comes with us shall bequeath the title of
Dawn Treader to all his descendants, and when we
land at Cair Paravel on the homeward voyage he
shall have either gold or land enough to make him
rich all his life. Now—scatter over the island, all
of you. In half an hour's time I shall receive the
names that Lord Drinian brings me."

There was rather a sheepish silence and then
the crew made their bows and moved away, one in
this direction and one in that, but mostly in little
knots or bunches, talking.

"And now for the Lord Rhoop," said Caspian.

But turning to the head of the table he saw that

Rhoop was already there. He had arrived, silent and unnoticed, while the discussion was going on, and was seated beside the Lord Argoz. The daughter of Ramandu stood beside him as if she had just helped him into his chair; Ramandu stood behind him and laid both his hands on Rhoop's gray head. Even in daylight a faint silver light came from the hands of the star. There was a smile on Rhoop's haggard face. He held out one of his hands to Lucy and the other to Caspian. For a moment it looked as if he were going to say something. Then his smile brightened as if he were feeling some delicious sensation, a long sigh of contentment came from his lips, his head fell forward, and he slept.

"Poor Rhoop," said Lucy. "I *am* glad. He must have had terrible times."

"Don't let's even think of it," said Eustace.

Meanwhile Caspian's speech, helped perhaps by some magic of the island, was having just the effect he intended. A good many who had been anxious enough to *get* out of the voyage felt quite differently about being *left* out of it. And of course whenever any one sailor announced that he had made up his mind to ask for permission to sail, the ones who hadn't said this felt that they were getting fewer and more uncomfortable. So that before the half-hour was nearly over several people were positively "sucking up" to Drinian and Rhince (at least that was what they called it at my school) to get a good report. And soon there were only three left who didn't want to go, and those three were trying very hard to persuade others to stay with them. And very shortly after that there was only one left. And in the end he began to be afraid of being left behind all on his own and changed his mind.

At the end of the half-hour they all came trooping back to Aslan's Table and stood at one end while Drinian and Rhince went and sat down with Caspian and made their report; and Caspian accepted all the men but that one who had changed his mind at the last moment. His name was Pittencream and he stayed on the Island of the Star all the time the others were away looking for the World's End, and he very much wished he had gone with them. He wasn't the sort of man who could enjoy talking to Ramandu and Ramandu's daughter (nor they to him), and it rained a good deal, and though there was a wonderful feast on the Table every night, he didn't very much enjoy it. He said it gave him the creeps sitting there alone (and in the rain as likely as not) with those four Lords asleep at the end of the Table. And when the others returned he felt so out of things that he deserted on the voyage home at the Lone Islands, and went and lived in Calormen, where he told wonderful stories about his adventures at the End of the World, until at last he came to believe them himself. So you may say, in a sense, that he lived happily ever after. But he could never bear mice.

That night they all ate and drank together at the great Table between the pillars where the feast was magically renewed: and next morning the *Dawn Treader* set sail once more just when the great birds had come and gone again.

"Lady," said Caspian, "I hope to speak with you again when I have broken the enchantments.' And Ramandu's daughter looked at him and smiled.

THE WONDERS
OF THE LAST SEA

VERY SOON AFTER THEY HAD LEFT
Ramandu's country they began to feel that they
had already sailed beyond the world. All was different. For one thing they all found that they were
needing less sleep. One did not want to go to bed
nor to eat much, nor even to talk except in low
voices. Another thing was the light. There was too
much of it. The sun when it came up each morning
looked twice, if not three times, its usual size. And
every morning (which gave Lucy the strangest
feeling of all) the huge white birds, singing their
song with human voices in a language no one
knew, streamed overhead and vanished astern on
their way to their breakfast at Aslan's Table. A little later they came flying back and vanished into
the east.

"How beautifully clear the water is!" said Lucy
to herself, as she leaned over the port side early in
the afternoon of the second day.

And it was. The first thing that she noticed was a little black object, about the size of a shoe, traveling along at the same speed as the ship. For a moment she thought it was something floating on the surface. But then there came floating past a bit of stale bread which the cook had just thrown out of the galley. And the bit of bread looked as if it were going to collide with the black thing, but it didn't. It passed above it, and Lucy now saw that the black thing could not be on the surface. Then the black thing suddenly got very much bigger and flicked back to normal size a moment later.

Now Lucy knew she had seen something just like that happen somewhere else—if only she could remember where. She held her hand to her head and screwed up her face and put out her tongue in the effort to remember. At last she did. Of course! It was like what you saw from a train on a bright sunny day. You saw the black shadow of your own coach running along the fields at the same pace as the train. Then you went into a cutting; and immediately the same shadow flicked close up to you and got big, racing along the grass of the cutting-bank. Then you came out of the cutting and—flick!—once more the black shadow had gone back to its normal size and was running along the fields.

"It's our shadow!—the shadow of the *Dawn Treader*," said Lucy. "Our shadow running along on the bottom of the sea. That time when it got bigger it went over a hill. But in that case the water must be clearer than I thought! Good gracious, I must be seeing the bottom of the sea; fathoms and fathoms down."

As soon as she had said this she realized that the great silvery expanse which she had been seeing (without noticing) for some time was really the sand on the sea-bed and that all sorts of darker or brighter patches were not lights and shadows on the surface but real things on the bottom. At present, for instance, they were passing over a mass of soft purply green with a broad, winding strip of pale gray in the middle of it. But now that she knew it was on the bottom she saw it much better. She could see that bits of the dark stuff were much higher than other bits and were waving gently. "Just like trees in a wind," said Lucy. "And I do believe that's what they are. It's a submarine forest."

They passed on above it and presently the pale streak was joined by another pale streak. "If I was down there," thought Lucy, "that streak would be just like a road through the wood. And that place where it joins the other would be a crossroads. Oh, I do wish I was. Hallo! the forest is coming to an end. And I do believe the streak really was a road! I can still see it going on across the open sand. It's a different color. And it's marked out with something at the edges—dotted lines. Perhaps they are stones. And now it's getting wider."

But it was not really getting wider, it was getting nearer. She realized this because of the way in which the shadow of the ship came rushing up toward her. And the road—she felt sure it was a road now—began to go in zigzags. Obviously it was climbing up a steep hill. And when she held her head sideways and looked back, what she saw was very like what you see when you look down a winding road from the top of a hill. She could even see the shafts of sunlight falling through the deep water onto the wooded valley—and, in the extreme distance, everything melting away into a dim greenness. But some places—the sunny ones, she thought—were ultramarine blue.

She could not, however, spend much time looking back; what was coming into view in the forward direction was too exciting. The road had apparently now reached the top of the hill and ran straight forward. Little specks were moving to and fro on it. And now something most wonderful, fortunately in full sunlight—or as full as it can be when it falls through fathoms of water—flashed into sight. It was knobbly and jagged and of a pearly, or perhaps an ivory, color. She was so nearly straight above it that at first she could hardly make out what it was. But everything became plain when she noticed its shadow. The sunlight was falling across Lucy's shoulders, so the shadow of the thing lay stretched out on the sand behind it. And by its shape she saw clearly that it was a shadow of towers and pinnacles, minarets and domes.

"Why!—it's a city or a huge castle," said Lucy to herself. "But I wonder why they've built it on top of a high mountain?"

Long afterward when she was back in England and talked all these adventures over with Edmund, they thought of a reason and I am pretty sure it is the true one. In the sea, the deeper you go, the darker and colder it gets, and it is down there, in the dark and cold, that dangerous things live—the squid and the Sea Serpent and the Kraken. The valleys are the wild, unfriendly places. The sea-people feel about their valleys as we do about mountains, and feel about their mountains as we feel about valleys. It is on the heights (or, as we would say, "in the shallows") that there is warmth and peace. The reckless hunters and brave knights of the sea go down into the depths on quests and adventures, but return home to the heights for rest and peace, courtesy and council, the sports, the dances and the songs.

They had passed the city and the sea-bed was still rising. It was only a few hundred feet below the ship now. The road had disappeared. They were sailing above an open park-like country, dotted with little groves of brightly-colored vegetation. And then—Lucy nearly squealed aloud with excitement—she had seen People.

There were between fifteen and twenty of them, and all mounted on sea-horses—not the tiny little sea-horses which you may have seen in museums but horses rather bigger than themselves. They must be noble and lordly people, Lucy thought, for she could catch the gleam of gold on some of their foreheads and streamers of emerald- or orange-colored stuff fluttered from their shoulders in the current. Then:

"Oh, bother these fish!" said Lucy, for a whole shoal of small fat fish, swimming quite close to the surface, had come between her and the Sea People. But though this spoiled her view it led to the most interesting thing of all. Suddenly a fierce little fish of a kind she had never seen before came darting up from below, snapped, grabbed, and sank rapidly with one of the fat fish in its mouth. And all the Sea People were sitting on their horses staring up at what had happened. They seemed to be talking and laughing. And before the hunting fish had got back to them with its prey, another of the same kind came up from the Sea People. And Lucy was almost certain that one big Sea Man who sat on his sea-horse in the middle of the party had sent it or released it; as if he had been holding it back till then in his hand or on his wrist.

"Why, I do declare," said Lucy, "it's a hunting

party. Or more like a hawking party. Yes, that's it. They ride out with these little fierce fish on their wrists just as we used to ride out with falcons on our wrists when we were Kings and Queens at Cair Paravel long ago. And then they fly them—or I suppose I should say *swim* them—at the others. How—"

She stopped suddenly because the scene was changing. The Sea People had noticed the *Dawn Treader*. The shoal of fish had scattered in every

direction: the People themselves were coming up to find out the meaning of this big, black thing which had come between them and the sun. And now they were so close to the surface that if they had been in air, instead of water, Lucy could have spoken to them. There were men and women both.

All wore coronets of some kind and many had chains of pearls. They wore no other clothes. Their bodies were the color of old ivory, their hair dark purple. The King in the center (no one could mistake him for anything but the King) looked proudly and fiercely into Lucy's face and shook a spear in his hand. His knights did the same. The faces of the ladies were filled with astonishment. Lucy felt sure they had never seen a ship or a human before—and how should they, in seas beyond the world's end where no ship ever came?

"What are you staring at, Lu?" said a voice close beside her.

Lucy had been so absorbed in what she was seeing that she started at the sound, and when she turned she found that her arm had gone "dead" from leaning so long on the rail in one position. Drinian and Edmund were beside her.

"Look," she said.

They both looked, but almost at once Drinian said in a low voice:

"Turn round at once, your Majesties—that's right, with our backs to the sea. And don't look as if we were talking about anything important."

"Why, what's the matter?" said Lucy as she obeyed.

"It'll never do for the sailors to see *all that*," said Drinian. "We'll have men falling in love with a sea-woman, or falling in love with the under-sea country itself, and jumping overboard. I've heard of that kind of thing happening before in strange seas. It's always unlucky to see *these* people."

"But we used to know them," said Lucy. "In the old days at Cair Paravel when my brother Peter was High King. They came to the surface and sang at our coronation."

"I think that must have been a different kind, Lu," said Edmund. "They could live in the air as well as under water. I rather think these can't. By the look of them they'd have surfaced and started attacking us long ago if they could. They seem very fierce."

"At any rate," began Drinian, but at that moment two sounds were heard. One was a plop. The other was a voice from the fighting-top shouting, "Man overboard!" Then everyone was busy. Some of the sailors hurried aloft to take in the sail; others hurried below to get to the oars; and Rhince, who was on duty on the poop, began to put the helm hard over so as to come round and back to the man who had gone overboard. But by now everyone knew that it wasn't strictly a man. It was Reepicheep.

"Drat that mouse!" said Drinian. "It's more trouble than all the rest of the ship's company put together. If there is any scrape to be got into, in it will get! It ought to be put in irons—keelhauled—marooned—have its whiskers cut off. Can anyone see the little blighter?"

All this didn't mean that Drinian really disliked Reepicheep. On the contrary he liked him very much and was therefore frightened about him, and being frightened put him in a bad temper—just as your mother is much angrier with you for running out into the road in front of a car than a stranger would be. No one, of course, was afraid of Reepicheep's drowning, for he was an excellent swimmer; but the three who knew what was going on below the water were afraid of those long, cruel spears in the hands of the Sea People.

In a few minutes the *Dawn Treader* had come round and everyone could see the black blob in the water which was Reepicheep. He was chattering with the greatest excitement but as his mouth kept on getting filled with water nobody could understand what he was saying.

"He'll blurt the whole thing out if we don't shut him up," cried Drinian. To prevent this he rushed to the side and lowered a rope himself, shouting to the sailors, "All right, all right. Back to your places. I hope I can heave a *mouse* up without help." And as Reepicheep began climbing up the rope—not very nimbly because his wet fur made him heavy—Drinian leaned over and whispered to him,

"Don't tell. Not a word."

But when the dripping Mouse had reached the deck it turned out not to be at all interested in the Sea People.

"Sweet!" he cheeped. "Sweet, sweet!"

"What are you talking about?" asked Drinian crossly. "And you needn't shake yourself all over *me*, either."

"I tell you the water's sweet," said the Mouse. "Sweet, fresh. It isn't salt."

For a moment no one quite took in the importance of this. But then Reepicheep once more repeated the old prophecy:

> "Where the waves grow sweet,
> Doubt not, Reepicheep,
> There is the utter East."

Then at last everyone understood.

"Let me have a bucket, Rynelf," said Drinian.

It was handed him and he lowered it and up it came again. The water shone in it like glass.

"Perhaps your Majesty would like to taste it first," said Drinian to Caspian.

The King took the bucket in both hands, raised it to his lips, sipped, then drank deeply and raised his head. His face was changed. Not only his eyes but everything about him seemed to be brighter.

"Yes," he said, "it is sweet. That's real water,

that. I'm not sure that it isn't going to kill me. But it is the death I would have chosen—if I'd known about it till now."

"What do you mean?" asked Edmund.

"It—it's like light more than anything else," said Caspian.

"That is what it is," said Reepicheep. "Drinkable light. We must be very near the end of the world now."

There was a moment's silence and then Lucy knelt down on the deck and drank from the bucket.

"It's the loveliest thing I have ever tasted," she said with a kind of gasp. "But oh—it's strong. We shan't need to *eat* anything now."

And one by one everybody on board drank. And for a long time they were all silent. They felt almost too well and strong to bear it; and presently they began to notice another result. As I have said before, there had been too much light ever since they left the island of Ramandu—the sun too large (though not too hot), the sea too bright, the air too shining. Now, the light grew no less—if anything, it increased—but they could bear it. They could look straight up at the sun without blinking. They could see more light than they had ever seen before. And the deck and the sail and their own faces and bodies became brighter and brighter and every rope shone. And next morning, when the sun rose, now five or six times its old size, they stared hard into it and could see the very feathers of the birds that came flying from it.

Hardly a word was spoken on board all that day, till about dinner-time (no one wanted any dinner, the water was enough for them) Drinian said:

"I can't understand this. There is not a breath of wind. The sail hangs dead. The sea is as flat as a pond. And yet we drive on as fast as if there were a gale behind us."

"I've been thinking that, too," said Caspian. "We must be caught in some strong current."

"H'm," said Edmund. "That's not so nice if the World really has an edge and we're getting near it."

"You mean," said Caspian, "that we might be just—well, poured over it?"

"Yes, yes," cried Reepicheep, clapping his paws together. "That's how I've always imagined it—the World like a great round table and the waters of all the oceans endlessly pouring over the edge. The ship will tip up—stand on her head—for one moment we shall see over the edge—and then, down, down, the rush, the speed—"

"And what do you think will be waiting for us at the bottom, eh?" said Drinian.

"Aslan's country, perhaps," said the Mouse, its eyes shining. "Or perhaps there isn't any bottom. Perhaps it goes down for ever and ever. But whatever it is, won't it be worth anything just to have looked for one moment beyond the edge of the world."

"But look here," said Eustace, "this is all rot. The world's round—I mean, round like a ball, not like a table."

"*Our* world is," said Edmund. "But is this?"

"Do you mean to say," asked Caspian, "that you three come from a round world (round like a ball) and you've never told me! It's really too bad of you. Because we have fairy-tales in which there are round worlds and I always loved them. I never believed there were any real ones. But I've always wished there were and I've always longed to live in one. Oh, I'd give anything—I wonder why you can get into our world and we never get into yours? If only I had the chance! It must be exciting to live on a thing like a ball. Have you ever been to the parts where people walk about upside-down?"

Edmund shook his head. "And it isn't like that," he added. "There's nothing particularly exciting about a round world when you're there."

Sixteen

THE VERY END
OF THE WORLD

REEPICHEEP WAS THE ONLY PERSON ON board besides Drinian and the two Pevensies who had noticed the Sea People. He had dived in at once when he saw the Sea King shaking his spear, for he regarded this as a sort of threat or challenge and wanted to have the matter out there and then. The excitement of discovering that the water was now fresh had distracted his attention, and before he remembered the Sea People again Lucy and Drinian had taken him aside and warned him not to mention what he had seen.

As things turned out they need hardly have bothered, for by this time the *Dawn Treader* was gliding over a part of the sea which seemed to be uninhabited. No one except Lucy saw anything more of the People, and even she had only one short glimpse. All morning on the following day they sailed in fairly shallow water and the bottom was weedy. Just before midday Lucy saw a large shoal of fishes grazing on the weed. They were all eating steadily and all moving in the same direction. "Just like a flock of sheep," thought Lucy. Suddenly she saw a little Sea Girl of about her own age in the middle of them—a quiet, lonely-looking girl with a sort of crook in her hand. Lucy felt sure that this girl must be a shepherdess—or perhaps a fish-herdess—and that the shoal was really a flock at pasture. Both the fishes and the girl were quite close to the surface. And just as the girl, gliding in the shallow water, and Lucy, leaning over the bulwark, came opposite to one another, the girl looked up and stared straight into Lucy's face. Neither could speak to the other and in a moment the Sea Girl dropped astern. But Lucy will never forget her face. It did not look frightened or angry like those of the other Sea People. Lucy had liked that girl and she felt certain the girl had liked her. In that one moment they had somehow become friends. There does not seem to be much chance of their meeting again in that world or any other. But if ever they do they will rush together with their hands held out.

After that for many days, without wind in her shrouds or foam at her bows, across a waveless sea, the *Dawn Treader* glided smoothly east. Every day and every hour the light became more brilliant and still they could bear it. No one ate or slept and no one wanted to, but they drew buckets of dazzling water from the sea, stronger than wine and somehow wetter, more liquid, than ordinary water, and pledged one another silently in deep drafts of it. And one or two of the sailors who had been oldish men when the voyage began now grew younger every day. Everyone on board was filled with joy and excitement, but not an excitement that made one talk. The further they sailed the less they spoke, and then almost in a whisper. The stillness of that last sea laid hold on them.

"My Lord," said Caspian to Drinian one day, "what do you see ahead?"

"Sire," said Drinian, "I see whiteness. All along the horizon from north to south, as far as my eyes can reach."

"That is what I see too," said Caspian, "and I cannot imagine what it is."

"If we were in higher latitudes, your Majesty," said Drinian, "I would say it was ice. But it can't be that; not here. All the same, we'd better get men to the oars and hold the ship back against the current. Whatever the stuff is, we don't want to crash into it at this speed!"

They did as Drinian said, and so continued to go slower and slower. The whiteness did not get any less mysterious as they approached it. If it was land it must be a very strange land, for it seemed just as smooth as the water and on the same level with it. When they got very close to it Drinian put the helm hard over and turned the *Dawn Treader* south so that she was broadside on to the current and rowed a little way southward along the edge of the whiteness. In so doing they accidentally made the important discovery that the current was only about forty feet wide and the rest of the sea as still as a pond. This was good news for the crew, who had already begun to think that the return journey to Ramandu's land, rowing against stream all the way, would be pretty poor sport. (It also explained why the shepherd girl had dropped so quickly astern. She was not in the current. If she had been she would have been moving east at the same speed as the ship.)

And still no one could make out what the white stuff was. Then the boat was lowered and it put off to investigate. Those who remained on the *Dawn Treader* could see that the boat pushed right in amidst the whiteness. Then they could hear the voices of the party in the boat (clear across the still water) talking in a shrill and surprised way. Then there was a pause while Rynelf in the bows of the boat took a sounding; and when, after that, the boat came rowing back there seemed to be plenty of the white stuff inside her. Everyone crowded to the side to hear the news.

"Lilies, your Majesty!" shouted Rynelf, standing up in the bows.

"*What* did you say?" asked Caspian.

"Blooming lilies, your Majesty," said Rynelf. "Same as in a pool or in a garden at home."

"Look!" said Lucy, who was in the stern of the boat. She held up her wet arms full of white petals and broad flat leaves.

"What's the depth, Rynelf?" asked Drinian.

"That's the funny thing, Captain," said Rynelf. "It's still deep. Three and a half fathoms clear."

"They can't be real lilies—not what we call lilies," said Eustace.

Probably they were not, but they were very like them. And when, after some consultation, the *Dawn Treader* turned back into the current and began to glide eastward through the Lily Lake or the Silver Sea (they tried both these names but it was the Silver Sea that stuck and is now on Caspian's map) the strangest part of their travels began. Very soon the open sea which they were leaving was only a thin rim of blue on the western horizon. Whiteness, shot with faintest color of gold, spread round them on every side, except just astern where their passage had thrust the lilies apart and left an open lane of water that shone like dark green glass. To look at, this last sea was very like the Arctic; and if their eyes had not by now grown as strong as eagles' the sun on all that whiteness—especially at early morning when the sun was hugest—would have been unbearable. And every evening the same whiteness made the daylight last longer. There seemed no end to the lilies. Day after day from all those miles and leagues of flowers there rose a smell which Lucy found it very hard to describe; sweet—yes, but not at all sleepy or overpowering, a fresh, wild, lonely smell that seemed to get into your brain and make you feel that you could go up mountains at a run or wrestle with an elephant. She and Caspian said to one another, "I feel that I can't stand much more of this, yet I don't want it to stop."

They took soundings very often but it was only several days later that the water became shallower. After that it went on getting shallower. There came a day when they had to row out of the current and feel their way forward at a snail's pace, rowing. And soon it was clear that the *Dawn Treader* could sail no further east. Indeed it was only by very clever handling that they saved her from grounding.

"Lower the boat," cried Caspian, "and then call the men aft. I must speak to them."

"What's he going to do?" whispered Eustace to Edmund. "There's a queer look in his eyes."

"I think we probably all look the same," said Edmund.

They joined Caspian on the poop and soon all the men were crowded together at the foot of the ladder to hear the King's speech.

"Friends," said Caspian, "we have now fulfilled

the quest on which you embarked. The seven lords are all accounted for and as Sir Reepicheep has sworn never to return, when you reach Ramandu's Land you will doubtless find the Lords Revilian and Argoz and Mavramorn awake. To you, my Lord Drinian, I entrust this ship, bidding you sail to Narnia with all the speed you may, and above all not to land on the Island of Deathwater. And instruct my regent, the Dwarf Trumpkin, to give to all these, my shipmates, the rewards I promised them. They have been earned well. And if I come not again it is my will that the Regent, and Master Cornelius, and Trufflehunter the Badger, and the Lord Drinian choose a King of Narnia with the consent—"

"But, Sire," interrupted Drinian, "are you abdicating?"

"I am going with Reepicheep to see the World's End," said Caspian.

A low murmur of dismay ran through the sailors.

"We will take the boat," said Caspian. "You will have no need of it in these gentle seas and you must build a new one on Ramandu's island. And now—"

"Caspian," said Edmund suddenly and sternly, "you can't do this."

"Most certainly," said Reepicheep, "his Majesty cannot."

"No indeed," said Drinian.

"Can't?" said Caspian sharply, looking for a moment not unlike his uncle Miraz.

"Begging your Majesty's pardon," said Rynelf from the deck below, "but if one of us did the same it would be called deserting."

"You presume too much on your long service, Rynelf," said Caspian.

"No, Sire! He's perfectly right," said Drinian.

"By the Mane of Aslan," said Caspian, "I had thought you were all my subjects here, not my schoolmasters."

"I'm not," said Edmund, "and I say you can *not* do this."

"Can't again," said Caspian. "What do you mean?"

"If it please your Majesty, we mean *shall not*," said Reepicheep with a very low bow. "You are the King of Narnia. You break faith with all your subjects, and especially with Trumpkin, if you do not return. You shall not please yourself with adventures as if you were a private person. And if your Majesty will not hear reason it will be the truest loyalty of every man on board to follow me in disarming and binding you till you come to your senses."

"Quite right," said Edmund. "Like they did with Ulysses when he wanted to go near the Sirens."

Caspian's hand had gone to his sword hilt, when Lucy said, "And you've almost promised

Ramandu's daughter to go back."

Caspian paused. "Well, yes. There is that," he said. He stood irresolute for a moment and then shouted out to the ship in general.

"Well, have your way. The quest is ended. We all return. Get the boat up again."

"Sire," said Reepicheep, "we do not *all* return. I, as I explained before—"

"Silence!" thundered Caspian. "I've been lessoned but I'll not be baited. Will no one silence that Mouse?"

"Your Majesty promised," said Reepicheep, "to be good lord to the Talking Beasts of Narnia."

"Talking beasts, yes," said Caspian. "I said nothing about beasts that never stop talking." And he flung down the ladder in a temper and went into the cabin, slamming the door.

But when the others rejoined him a little later they found him changed; he was white and there were tears in his eyes.

"It's no good," he said. "I might as well have behaved decently for all the good I did with my temper and swagger. Aslan has spoken to me. No—I don't mean he was actually here. He wouldn't fit into the cabin, for one thing. But that gold lion's head on the wall came to life and spoke to me. It was terrible—his eyes. Not that he was at all rough with me—only a bit stern at first. But it was terrible all the same. And he said—he said—oh, I can't bear it. The worst thing he could have said. You're to go on—Reep and Edmund, and Lucy, and Eustace; and I'm to go back. Alone. And at once. And what *is* the good of anything?"

"Caspian, dear," said Lucy. "You knew we'd have to go back to our own world sooner or later."

"Yes," said Caspian with a sob, "but this is sooner."

"You'll feel better when you get back to Ramandu's Island," said Lucy.

He cheered up a little later on, but it was a grievous parting on both sides and I will not dwell on it. About two o'clock in the afternoon, well victualed and watered (though they thought they would need neither food nor drink) and with Reepicheep's coracle on board, the boat pulled away from the *Dawn Treader* to row through the endless carpet of lilies. The *Dawn Treader* flew all her flags and hung out her shields to honor their departure. Tall and big and homelike she looked from their low position with the lilies all round them. And even before she was out of sight they saw her turn and begin rowing slowly westward. Yet though Lucy shed a few tears, she could not feel it as much as you might have expected. The light, the silence, the tingling smell of the Silver Sea, even (in some odd way) the loneliness itself, were too exciting.

There was no need to row, for the current

drifted them steadily to the east. None of them slept or ate. All that night and all next day they glided eastward, and when the third day dawned— with a brightness you or I could not bear even if we had dark glasses on—they saw a wonder ahead. It was as if a wall stood up between them and the sky, a greenish-gray, trembling, shimmering wall. Then up came the sun, and at its first rising they saw it through the wall and it turned into wonderful rainbow colors. Then they knew that the wall was really a long, tall wave—a wave endlessly fixed in one place as you may often see at the edge of a waterfall. It seemed to be about thirty feet high, and the current was gliding them swiftly toward it. You might have supposed they would have thought of their danger. They didn't. I don't think anyone could have in their position. For now they saw something not only behind the wave but behind the sun. They could not have seen even the sun if their eyes had not been strengthened by the water of the Last Sea. But now they could look at the rising sun and see it clearly and see things beyond it. What they saw—eastward, beyond the sun—was a range of mountains. It was so high that either they never saw the top of it or they forgot it. None of them remembers seeing any sky in that direction. And the mountains must really have been outside the world. For any mountains even a quarter of a twentieth of that height ought to have had ice and snow on them. But these were warm and green and full of forests and waterfalls however high you looked. And suddenly there came a breeze from the east, tossing the top of the wave into foamy shapes and ruffling the smooth water all round them. It lasted only a second or so but what it brought them in that second none of those three children will ever forget. It brought both a smell and a sound, a musical sound. Edmund and Eustace would never talk about it afterward. Lucy could only say, "It would break your heart." "Why," said I, "was it so sad?" "Sad!! No," said Lucy.

No one in that boat doubted that they were

seeing beyond the End of the World into Aslan's country.

At that moment, with a crunch, the boat ran aground. The water was too shallow now for it. "This," said Reepicheep, "is where I go on alone."

They did not even try to stop him, for everything now felt as if it had been fated or had happened before. They helped him to lower his little coracle. Then he took off his sword ("I shall need it no more," he said) and flung it far away across the lilied sea. Where it fell it stood upright with the hilt above the surface. Then he bade them good-bye, trying to be sad for their sakes; but he was quivering with happiness. Lucy, for the first and last time, did what she had always wanted to do, taking him in her arms and caressing him. Then hastily he got into his coracle and took his paddle, and the current caught it and away he went, very black against the lilies. But no lilies grew on the wave; it was a smooth green slope. The coracle went more and more quickly, and beautifully it rushed up the wave's side. For one split second they saw its shape and Reepicheep's on the very top. Then it vanished, and since that moment no one can truly claim to have seen Reepicheep the Mouse. But my belief is that he came safe to Aslan's country and is alive there to this day.

As the sun rose the sight of those mountains

outside the world faded away. The wave remained but there was only blue sky behind it.

The children got out of the boat and waded— not toward the wave but southward with the wall of water on their left. They could not have told you why they did this; it was their fate. And though they had felt—and been—very grown-up on the *Dawn Treader*, they now felt just the opposite and held hands as they waded through the lilies. They never felt tired. The water was warm and all the time it got shallower. At last they were on dry sand, and then on grass—a huge plain of very fine short grass, almost level with the Silver Sea and spreading in every direction without so much as a molehill.

And of course, as it always does in a perfectly flat place without trees, it looked as if the sky came down to meet the grass in front of them. But as they went on they got the strangest impression that here at last the sky did really come down and join the earth—a blue wall, very bright, but real and solid: more like glass than anything else. And soon they were quite sure of it. It was very near now.

But between them and the foot of the sky there was something so white on the green grass that even with their eagles' eyes they could hardly look at it. They came on and saw that it was a Lamb.

"Come and have breakfast," said the Lamb in

its sweet milky voice.

Then they noticed for the first time that there was a fire lit on the grass and fish roasting on it. They sat down and ate the fish, hungry now for

the first time for many days. And it was the most delicious food they had ever tasted.

"Please, Lamb," said Lucy, "is this the way to Aslan's country?"

"Not for you," said the Lamb. "For you the door into Aslan's country is from your own world."

"What!" said Edmund. "Is there a way into Aslan's country from our world too?"

"There is a way into my country from all the worlds," said the Lamb; but as he spoke his snowy white flushed into tawny gold and his size changed and he was Aslan himself, towering above them and scattering light from his mane.

"Oh, Aslan," said Lucy. "Will you tell us how to get into your country from our world?"

"I shall be telling you all the time," said Aslan. "But I will not tell you how long or short the way will be; only that it lies across a river. But do not fear that, for I am the great Bridge Builder. And now come; I will open the door in the sky and send you to your own land."

"Please, Aslan," said Lucy. "Before we go, will you tell us when we can come back to Narnia again? Please. And oh, do, do, do make it soon."

"Dearest," said Aslan very gently, "you and your brother will never come back to Narnia."

"Oh, *Aslan*!!" said Edmund and Lucy both together in despairing voices.

"You are too old, children," said Aslan, "and you must begin to come close to your own world now."

"It isn't Narnia, you know," sobbed Lucy. "It's *you*. We shan't meet *you* there. And how can we live, never meeting you?"

"But you shall meet me, dear one," said Aslan.

"Are—are you there too, Sir?" said Edmund.

"I am," said Aslan. "But there I have another name. You must learn to know me by that name. This was the very reason why you were brought to Narnia, that by knowing me here for a little, you may know me better there."

"And is Eustace never to come back here either?" said Lucy.

"Child," said Aslan, "do you really need to know that? Come, I am opening the door in the sky." Then all in one moment there was a rending of the blue wall (like a curtain being torn) and a terrible white light from beyond the sky, and the feel of Aslan's mane and a Lion's kiss on their foreheads and then—the back bedroom in Aunt Alberta's home at Cambridge.

Only two more things need to be told. One is that Caspian and his men all came safely back to Ramandu's Island. And the three lords woke from their sleep. Caspian married Ramandu's daughter and they all reached Narnia in the end, and she became a great queen and the mother and grandmother of great kings. The other is that back in our own world everyone soon started saying how Eustace had improved, and how "You'd never know him for the same boy": everyone except Aunt Alberta, who said he had become very commonplace and tiresome and it must have been the influence of those Pevensie children.

Teacher's Guide to
THE CHRONICLES OF NARNIA
by C. S. Lewis

CONTENTS

INTRODUCING *THE CHRONICLES OF NARNIA*

ABOUT *THE CHRONICLES OF NARNIA*

Narnia . . . where the adventure begins. In this series of exciting stories, children who get into the fantasy world of Narnia must time and again test their bravery and capacity for belief in order to come to the aid of others—and to learn more about themselves. *The Chronicles of Narnia* are filled with fascinating and fanciful characters—talking animals, dancing trees, evil witches, and creatures wholly of the author's imagination. Readers who enter this enchanted world meet these creatures in richly imagined settings and distinctly different lands, brought there by magic along with the children who stumble across the mysterious portals connecting our world with theirs.

The Chronicles of Narnia are among the world's best-known fantasies—stories of imagination in which the action often depends on magic or the supernatural. They are part of the classic fantasy genre that includes Lewis Carroll's *Alice's Adventures in Wonderland* and J. R. R. Tolkien's *The Hobbit*.

The seven books of *The Chronicles of Narnia* were published between 1950 and 1956. *The Lion, the Witch and the Wardrobe* came first—it was because of the popularity of this book that the other books were written. But the author later expressed a wish that the books be sequenced by Narnian chronology, rather than the order in which they were first published. Thus the series now begins with *The Magician's Nephew*, in which the world of Narnia is created, and ends with *The Last Battle*, in which it is destroyed—so that a new world can begin.

ABOUT C. S. LEWIS (1898–1963)

As a young child, C. S. Lewis used to hide with his brother in a dark wardrobe, where they told each other stories. When he was eight years old they made up a land called Boxen, where talking animals lived. Years later, these experiences helped inspire Lewis to write one of the most popular children's series of all time, *The Chronicles of Narnia*.

Clive Staples (known to his friends as Jack) Lewis was born in Belfast, Ireland. After attending Oxford University and serving in World War I, he became a university Fellow, writing many books on literature, religion, and philosophy. As bombs devastated London during World War II, four children came to live with Lewis in his country home. He decided to write them a story, and the world of Narnia was born. In these books, Lewis combined classic elements of fantasy—fanciful creatures and imaginary lands—with representations of good versus evil.

SHARING *THE CHRONICLES OF NARNIA*

READING SKILLS AND STRATEGIES	THEMES
Analyze Structure	Beliefs
Examine Voice and Viewpoint	Courage
Investigate Character	Decision Making
Keep a Journal	Fantasy
Recognize Literary Devices	Power

READING SKILLS AND STRATEGIES

Analyze Structure

Have students look at how the author uses digressions, stories within stories, flashbacks, and shifts in point of view to convey information and keep the story moving. What role does suspense play in the stories? How is it created and sustained? Students should be aware that part of an author's art is deciding what to omit. Watch for what Lewis tells us he isn't telling us!

Examine Voice and Viewpoint

Ask students to consider the following questions: Who is the narrator of *The Chronicles of Narnia*? What words would students use to describe the narrator's voice? How does the author use humor and irony to entertain the reader, and what effect do these have on the story? Ask students to take special note of asides to the audience, places where the narrator breaks the story to talk directly to the reader. What do these moments add to the story?

Investigate Character

Have students analyze the characters they encounter in *The Chronicles of Narnia.* They may consider their traits, motivations, conflicts, points of view, relationships, and the changes they undergo. How is C. S. Lewis able to establish character with a few carefully chosen details? How does character affect action? Can we tell what a character will do in a given situation based on what we know about him or her? When do characters change, and why? How do recurring characters evolve over the course of *The Chronicles of Narnia?*

Keep a Journal

Students can keep journals to record their responses to the books as they read. You might ask students to use journals to do any or all of the following:

• Pause at points when characters face a difficult decision and ask themselves: What would I do in this situation?

• Choose a character who speaks in a distinct style and write a paragraph in that character's voice.

• Choose a character whose point of view is not shown in a particular section and tell the section's story from that character's point of view.

• Record questions you would like to ask the author or the characters.

• Note literary devices; keep lists of new vocabulary words.

• Write down quotations you find interesting and might like to discuss later. In particular, you could note observations that you think apply to *our* world.

• Sketch drawings inspired by mental images the text evokes.

Recognize Literary Devices

Lewis's lively writing provides repeated opportunities to identify wordplay, analogies, similes, metaphors, allegories, and symbolism. Ask students to be aware of how different characters use language. How do these devices enrich the text?

THEMES

Beliefs

Characters regularly confront issues of good and evil. How does what a character believes affect how he or she acts and vice versa? What are some examples of good and evil behavior? How do the characters respond to good and evil?

Courage

What is courage? When do characters show courage? Have students examine the difference between rash action and courageous action. What is the difference between caution and cowardice? How does fear affect how the characters perceive the world, and how they act?

Decision Making

Throughout *The Chronicles of Narnia*, characters face difficult choices. Ask students to pause periodically in their reading to reflect on what they would do in a particular character's situation. As they continue reading, have them note which tactics lead to successful resolutions.

Fantasy

Have students discuss the different elements that make up fantasy. What images of this fantasy world are most vivid? How do the children adapt to the altered realities of Narnia? What preconceptions do they bring with them?

Power

Have students discuss the meaning of power. Why do people want power? How does a good ruler use power? How is power sometimes misused?

DISCUSSIONS ACROSS *THE CHRONICLES OF NARNIA*

The following questions are designed to spark discussion about the issues and topics raised in this series.

Childhood and Adulthood

"Children have one kind of silliness, as you know, and grown-ups have another kind." (*The Magician's Nephew*, p. 89) How would you describe the difference between these kinds of silliness? What are some other observations the author makes about children and adults? Do you think Lewis remembered his own childhood or had a sense of how children think? Why or why not?

Complexity of Emotion

Lewis frequently shows characters feeling more than

one thing at once, or experiencing closely alternating emotions. Find examples of this in the books and see if you can explain the characters' experience. Can you think of a time when you felt two different ways about something in your own life?

Gender Roles

Compare male and female roles in the books. How do *The Chronicles of Narnia* reflect different expectations for boys and girls? How do attitudes about gender roles at the time the series was written (early to mid-1950s) compare with attitudes now?

Recurring Characters

Which characters were your favorites? Why do you think the author decides to send particular characters—and not others—on each specific voyage?

Talking and Non-Talking Animals

What distinction is made between talking animals and non-talking animals? Why do Narnians consider it horrible to kill or eat a talking animal when it is okay to kill or eat a non-talking one? What does this say about the importance of speech to the author, or as an attribute of humanity?

INDEPENDENT PROJECTS

You may not have time to read all of *The Chronicles of Narnia* with your class. If not, you might want to encourage students to continue reading the books on their own. Following are suggestions for independent projects for your students who read the whole series.

Create a Values Chart

Make a chart with two columns, "Values" and "Characters." In the first column list the following values represented in *The Chronicles of Narnia*: charity, faith, humility, justice, mercy. In the second column list the characters in whom you see these values embodied.

Make a Narnia Map

Create a map of the world of Narnia, showing its physical features, towns, and other places of interest. You may want to include drawings of some of the characters and events.

Make a Narnian Timeline

Narnian time moves differently from ours, and you learn a little more about this in each book. Make two parallel timelines showing how much time has passed between the books—in Narnia and in England.

Research Historical Connections

The Chronicles of Narnia were written in the years following the cataclysmic events of World War II. In fact, the first Narnia book—*The Lion, the Witch and the Wardrobe*—takes place while bombs are falling on London. Research why the Allied defeat of the Nazis has been viewed as the triumph of good over evil.

Then write a report describing how the historical events of World War II may have played a role in *The Chronicles of Narnia*, especially in the ongoing struggle between Narnia and Calormen.

Write a Character Study
Choose two characters who appear in several books. Write a character study of each describing how he or she grows and develops from one book to the next.

Write a Descriptive Poem
From its creation in *The Magician's Nephew* to its destruction in *The Last Battle*, the world of Narnia is revealed in increasingly detailed layers. Write a poem evoking the physical world of Narnia.

Write a Fantasy
C. S. Lewis used the genre of fantasy to create a world in which characters must regularly confront issues of good and evil, right and wrong. Write your own fantasy. Create a world based wholly on your own imagination, filled with fanciful creatures facing conflicts that test their morality.

Write a One-Act Play
Select a scene from one of the books and rewrite it as a one-act play. Describe the setting and write new dialogue as needed. Be sure your play reflects the viewpoints of the characters as presented in the book.

Write an Interview
Suppose you could interview C. S. Lewis. Write questions about the books and then, based on your reading of *The Chronicles of Narnia*, the answers you think he would give.

BOOK 1
THE MAGICIAN'S NEPHEW
**"Narnia, Narnia, Narnia, awake. Love.
Think. Speak. Be walking trees.
Be talking beasts. Be divine
waters."** (p. 126)

SETTING THE SCENE
Narnia—where the woods are thick and cool and where Talking Beasts are called to life—a new world where the adventure begins.

Digory's uncle Andrew has used dust from another world to fashion magic rings that he himself is afraid to use to explore other worlds. But when Digory and his new friend Polly stumble into Uncle Andrew's attic, the magician is not afraid to try the rings on the children! Digory and Polly are then drawn into worlds beyond our own, where they find many unexpected adventures. When Digory's action in one world awakens a witch from a spell, the children's travel between the worlds takes on a new urgency, to stop the witch in her quest for power.

QUESTIONS FOR GROUP DISCUSSION

• What are some of the different ways Lewis allows us to discover the characters? For example, what do we learn from how they appear, how they act and react, what they say, and how they contrast with one another?

• How does Lewis create a sense of place as the characters arrive in new worlds? Through whose point of view are new places described?

• What is the Wood Between the Worlds? What effect does it have on Polly and Digory? On the Witch and Uncle Andrew? Why? What do you think the Wood symbolizes?

WHAT WOULD YOU DO?
"Make your choice, adventurous Stranger;
Strike the bell and bide the danger,
Or wonder, till it drives you mad,
What would have followed if you had."
(p. 54)

First review and describe the different reactions Digory and Polly have to this challenge. Then consider: Which choice would you make? Would you rather have the danger and the definite answer—or the safety and the lingering question?

Digory is sent on a mission to bring back an apple that will protect Narnia. The same apple can restore health to his mother. What do you think you would do if someone you loved was sick and you were given a chance to save him or her, but you had to break an important rule to do so?

• One of the first experiences that enters Narnia, after Aslan sings it to life, is laughter. Why do you think the author decided to establish Narnia with a joke?

• Why do you think Aslan sends Digory for the apple, when he could easily make it appear?

• What does the choice of the Cabby as the first King of Narnia seem to say about the attributes of a good ruler?

DISCUSS QUOTES

Explain the following quotations. What do they mean in context? What do you think of the ideas expressed?

• "Men like me, who possess hidden wisdom, are freed from common rules just as we are cut off from common pleasures. Ours, my boy, is a high and lonely destiny." (Uncle Andrew, p. 21)

• "Things always work according to their nature. She has won her heart's desire; she has unwearying strength and endless days like a goddess. But length of days with an evil heart is only length of misery and already she begins to know it. All get what they want; they do not always like it." (Aslan, p. 190)

JOURNAL WRITING: Sensory Images

"But it was a different kind of quietness. The silence of the Wood had been rich and warm (you could almost hear the trees growing) and full of life: this was a dead, cold, empty silence." (p. 47) Listen for a quiet moment. Then describe the quiet.

BOOK 2

THE LION, THE WITCH AND THE WARDROBE
**"Once there were four children whose names were
Peter, Susan, Edmund and Lucy."** (p. 1)

SETTING THE SCENE

Narnia—the land beyond the wardrobe, the secret
country known only to Peter, Susan, Edmund, and
Lucy—the place where the adventure begins.

Four siblings journey from London during World War
II to stay at an unusual home in the English
countryside. Through a forgotten wardrobe filled with
musty coats, the children find the enchanted land of
Narnia. A secret world of magic and danger, Narnia is
ruthlessly ruled by the White Witch, who has cast the
land into an eternal winter. Only the return of the
Great Lion, Aslan, can break the Witch's evil spell.
And a rumor is spreading: Aslan is on his way back.
It is at this turbulent moment that the four children
stumble through the wardrobe and find themselves
center stage in the battle for control of Narnia.

QUESTIONS FOR GROUP DISCUSSION

• What are some individual character traits of each of
  the four children: Peter, Susan, Edmund, and Lucy?
  How do they change over the course of the story?

• Compare and contrast the characters of the Lion and
  the Witch (for example, what kinds of power they
  have, how they exercise power, how they treat

others, what they want).

• What do you think is the most courageous act shown in this book? Explain.

• Why do you think Edmund lies about having been to Narnia? How does lying affect him?

• In what ways is the Professor an unusual grown-up? What do you think about his "logic"? (see p. 48)

WHAT WOULD YOU DO?
"If it comes to that, which *is* the right side? How do we know that the Fauns are in the right and the Queen . . . is in the wrong? We don't really know anything about either." (Edmund, p. 62)

What do you think the answer is? How do you know right from wrong—and if you don't know, how do you decide what to do?

At the end of the book, the children become Kings and Queens of Narnia. Reread the description of some of the things they did during their reign (p. 183). If you suddenly found yourself ruler of a land, what would you do? What laws would you make? What goals would you try to reach?

• How does Edmund justify his choice to go to the White Witch? Why do you think people make up excuses for doing something that deep inside they know is wrong?

• Why do you think Aslan chooses not to resist as he is dragged and bound by the White Witch's creatures, even though "one of those paws could have been the death of them all"? (p. 153) How might the Lion's sacrifice function as an allegory?

• What do you think of the Professor's advice to the children at the end of the book? What message might the author be sending to the reader?

EXPLORE LANGUAGE

The Lion, the Witch and the Wardrobe is written in a friendly, informal voice, in the idiom of 1940s Britain. Therefore, occasional words and phrases may be unfamiliar to American students. Examples in the first chapter include the words "wardrobe" (closet where clothes are kept), "wireless" (radio, p. 5), and "looking-glass" (mirror, p. 6). As students read, ask them to write down words and expressions that seem to come from a different time or place. Then have them work in small groups to discuss what these expressions mean and to create a two-column "translation" chart in which they include definitions in familiar "American" English.

Lewis is wonderful at creating analogies, at helping readers understand something they don't know by comparing it to something they might know. Examples include the long description of the ride on the Lion's back (p. 164) or of the statues coming to life again (pp. 167–8). Challenge students to think of something they have done or seen that others may not have experienced. Then have volunteers try to come up with a way to describe this to someone by comparing it to something that would be more familiar to them.

JOURNAL WRITING: Write a Fantasy

Imagine you slipped through a secret passage into another world. Make up a fantasy about meeting someone there. Write about what happens and how you get back.

BOOK 3
THE HORSE AND HIS BOY
"Why, I might be anyone!" (p. 10)

SETTING THE SCENE

Narnia—where horses talk and hermits like company—the place where the adventure begins. It's Narnia's Golden Age, when Peter is High King.

A boy named Shasta and a talking horse named Bree—separately captured in youth and enslaved in Calormen—together attempt to make their escape to Narnia, a land the horse dimly recalls and the boy does not know at all. Soon they meet another pair of fugitives—a Calormene girl named Aravis, escaping an arranged marriage, and her talking horse, Hwin. Their escape route takes them through the wondrous city of Tashbaan, where they find themselves in the midst of a larger adventure. It falls to them to save the lands to the North—Archenland and Narnia—from a surprise attack by the Calormenes. In the process, Shasta learns who he really is and even finds his real father.

QUESTIONS FOR GROUP DISCUSSION

• Why do you think Bree decides to talk to Shasta, after years of hiding the fact that he is a talking horse?

• What mistakes do Shasta and Aravis make about each other and why?

• In what different ways do the characters show pride? How does this help them? How does this hurt them?

• Why do you think the book is called *The Horse and His Boy* rather than *A Boy and His Horse*? Find places in the text where Shasta appears to be Bree's boy.

• What kind of leader is The Tisroc? How do we know? Why do you think he agrees to Prince Rabadash's plan?

• What are some words used to describe Aslan in this book? How is he able to be such different things at the same time? How do people react after they see Aslan? Why do you think Aslan tears Aravis's back?

• Why do you think Lewis decides to narrate the battle at Anvard through the Hermit's reflecting pool rather than at the scene or through Shasta's perspective? What tone does this lend the battle?

• Is Prince Rabadash's punishment appropriate? Why or why not?

THINKING ABOUT DIFFICULT QUESTIONS

How do cultural differences, and the perception of cultural differences, play a role in the relations between the people of Calormen and the people of the lands to the North? Find examples in the text of how rumors and prejudices are fed by limited information. How might European history and culture account for some of the attitudes reflected in the book?

DISCUSS QUOTES

Explain the following quotations. What do they mean in context? What do you think of the ideas expressed?

• "These little barbarian countries that call themselves *free* (which is as much to say, idle, disordered, and unprofitable) are hateful to the gods and to all persons of discernment." (The Tisroc, p. 112)

• "But as long as you know you're nobody very special, you'll be a very decent sort of Horse, on the whole . . ." (the Hermit, p. 152)

JOURNAL WRITING: Language

People have different ways of speaking in this book, depending on where they are from and what their position is in society. Choose a character and "translate" what he or she is saying into your own words or into language another character might use.

BOOK 4
PRINCE CASPIAN

"All you have heard about Old Narnia is true. It is not the land of Men. It is the country of Aslan, the country of the Waking Trees and Visible Naiads, of Fauns and Satyrs, of Dwarfs and Giants, of the gods and the Centaurs, of Talking Beasts. . . . The King does not allow them to be spoken of." (p. 51)

SETTING THE SCENE
Narnia—where animals talk and where magical things happen—where the adventure begins.

In a dreary train station in England on their way back to boarding school, Peter, Susan, Edmund, and Lucy suddenly feel themselves being tugged into another world. They arrive on an unknown island where they find the ancient ruins of a palace. But something feels familiar about this place. Eventually the children recognize that they are at Cair Paravel, where they themselves ruled as Queens and Kings of Narnia. They discover that they have been called back to Narnia because the forces of Old Narnia are in trouble. Just one year has passed in our world, but hundreds of years have passed in Narnia. The rightful king, Prince Caspian, is fighting a war against his uncle, King

Miraz, who wants to destroy the country of Aslan—the talking beasts and trees, the dwarfs and fauns—and all memory of Old Narnia. In desperation, Caspian's forces have blown a magical horn—the very horn Susan once received from Aslan—to summon the Lion and the children to help them in their struggle.

QUESTIONS FOR GROUP DISCUSSION

• Once more we meet Peter, Susan, Edmund, and Lucy. In what ways have they stayed the same? In what ways have they changed? How have their previous adventures shaped them? How do they behave differently as children and then as Kings and Queens of Narnia?

• Compare and contrast Nikabrik and Trufflehunter. What different points of view do they represent?

• "But because they have quarreled with the trees they are afraid of the woods. And because they are afraid of the woods they imagine that they are full of ghosts." (p. 55) What observation about fear does this reflect? Why do you think King Miraz is afraid of the stories of Old Narnia?

• How does faith or lack of faith guide the actions of characters in this book? What difficulties face a person who believes in something others cannot see? How does Susan feel when she does not follow Aslan? What does Aslan mean by telling her she has "listened to fears"? What do you think is the author's view of faith?

- What do you think of the way Peter faces the possibility that he might be killed by Miraz?

- In what way does Aslan test Caspian about his suitability to be King? How does Caspian pass the test?

- How does Reepicheep earn his tail back? Do you think he deserves this?

> **WHAT WOULD YOU DO?**
> Aslan implies that Lucy should have followed him, even if the others would not follow her. What would you do in this situation?

DISCUSS QUOTES
Explain the following quotations. What do they mean in context? What do you think of the ideas expressed?

- "I'll believe in anyone or anything . . . that'll batter these cursed Telmarine barbarians to pieces or drive them out of Narnia. Anyone or anything, Aslan *or* the White Witch, do you understand?" (Nikabrik, p. 77)

- "Wouldn't it be dreadful if some day in our own world, at home, men started going wild inside, like the animals here, and still looked like men, so that you'd never know which were which?" (Lucy, p. 122)

JOURNAL WRITING: Mental Images
Reread Lucy's thoughts on pages 117–8 about the trees coming to life. If a tree you have seen could come to life what do you think it would be like? How would

it move? How would it speak? What would it do? Write or draw your answer.

BOOK 5
THE VOYAGE OF THE DAWN TREADER
"My son," said the star, "it would be no use . . . to sail for the World's End with men unwilling or men deceived. That is not how great unenchantments are achieved." (p. 210)

SETTING THE SCENE
Narnia—where anything can happen, and usually does—and where the adventure begins.

Eustace Clarence Scrubb complains a lot. He also makes fun of the Narnia stories he hears his cousins Lucy and Edmund discussing. His point of view changes, however, when the three children are suddenly drawn up into a painting of a ship and find themselves swimming in the cold ocean waters off Narnia. There they are rescued by Prince Caspian and the crew of the *Dawn Treader*, who are on a mission to find the seven good lords banished from Narnia by the former King, Miraz. Meeting adventures at every island, the *Dawn Treader* travels beyond known lands, urged on by Prince Caspian's vow to find his father's friends and by the mouse Reepicheep, who longs to sail all the way into Aslan's country at the End of the World.

QUESTIONS FOR GROUP DISCUSSION

• *Eustace Clarence Scrubb:* Who is he in the beginning? Choose a fact or story about Eustace and explain what it tells us about him. How does he change as a result of his experiences on (and off) the *Dawn Treader*?

• *Reepicheep:* Why do you think he is so concerned with honor? How do you think being small (and a mouse) affects his behavior? Describe some contradictions in his personality. What does he do that's surprising? Why do you think he longs to sail to the End of the World?

• Examine how point of view shifts throughout this book. Locate some of the choices the author makes about whose point of view to tell a particular story from, and explain why you think he has chosen that character at that point.

• Talk about what happens to the characters and what they learn on the separate islands.
    —*Dragon Island*: Why do you think the author chose to have Eustace change specifically to a dragon?
    —*Deathwater Island*: Why do you think Reepicheep gives this name to the waters that turn things to gold?
    —Of which island does Caspian say, "There are some things no man can face?" (p. 198, the Island where Dreams come true) Why does he believe this?

• Edmund says to Ramandu's daughter: "When I look in

your face I can't help believing all you say: but then that's just what might happen with a witch too. How are we to know you're a friend?" She replies, "You can't know. . . . You can only believe—or not." (p. 201) What do you think of this answer? In a world of enchantment, how do you know whom to trust?

• How does Caspian convince the crew to continue the voyage with him to the World's End? How is he able to change the terms of the argument so that the crew members are eager to be included?

WHAT WOULD YOU DO?

There are several points at which Caspian has to decide whether to go on or turn back. Remember that once he passes the Lone Islands he does not even know if there is any land ahead. Reepicheep keeps urging them onward for the sake of adventure. Others want to turn back. What do you think you would advise if you were there, and why?

Reading Coriakin's magic book, Lucy is tempted to try the spell that lets you know what your friends really think of you. Would you be tempted by this spell? Why or why not?

• Explain the effect the Last Sea has on the crew of the *Dawn Treader* and on the children. "Everyone on board was filled with joy and excitement, but not an excitement that made one talk. The further they sailed the less they spoke, and then almost in a whisper. The stillness of that last sea laid hold on them." (p. 234) What is your understanding of this experience?

JOURNAL WRITING: Dealing with Fear

Throughout the book, look at what makes people afraid. How does fear make people act? How do things look different when people are not afraid of them? Keep this theme in mind as you read and record observations in your journal.

BOOK 6

THE SILVER CHAIR

"Pole, I say, are you good at believing things? I mean things that everyone here would laugh at?" "I've never had the chance," said Jill, "but I think I would be." (p. 6)

SETTING THE SCENE

Narnia—where a prince is put under an evil spell—and where the adventure begins.

To escape from bullies at school, Eustace and Jill run through a door in a wall—and come out into another world. Aslan has a job for them: to rescue Narnia's lost Prince. The only son of King Caspian, Prince Rilian disappeared in pursuit of a serpent, and no one in Narnia knows what happened to him. But Aslan gives Jill signs, which—if she is able to remember and follow carefully—will help her and Eustace find the Lost Prince. The children's journey takes them through the land of dangerous Giants, and on into underground caverns, where they finally encounter the Queen of the Deep Realm—and the knight she has enchanted. In this world far below the earth, the witch tries to convince them all that no other world exists . . . and she almost succeeds.

QUESTIONS FOR GROUP DISCUSSION

• Examine the characters.

—*Jill*: In what ways is she different from the other children who have gone to Narnia?

—*Eustace*: How has he changed since his last visit to Narnia?

—*Puddleglum*: Why does he always act as if the worst will happen? Does he believe it will? Are there any times when his attitude is helpful? How does the way he talks about himself differ from the way others perceive him?

• What do you think of the way Aslan behaves toward Jill when she first encounters him by the river? What is he trying to get her to learn, or to acknowledge?

• Look for places where stories are told within the story. Explain how this device is used to slow down or speed up the story, to show different points of view, and to get information across. How does the credibility of the speaker affect the way we receive the information?

• Find examples of times when characters act unafraid although they really are afraid. When is this a foolish thing to do? When is it necessary?

• How does Jill use expected "girlish" behavior to get what she really wants from the Giants? How can people use other people's mistaken expectations of them to their own advantage?

• Why does the witch try to enchant the characters into believing there is no Overworld? For what might this be an allegory?

• Reread Puddleglum's speech beginning, "Suppose we *have* only dreamed, or made up, all those things— trees and grass and sun and moon and stars and Aslan himself," continuing through "I'm going to live as like a Narnian as I can even if there isn't any Narnia." (p. 182) How does this argument lead to victory over the witch?

• How do the children finally get revenge on the bullies at school in their own world? Do you find this a satisfying ending? Why or why not?

WHAT WOULD YOU DO?

The Knight makes the children promise not to cut the cords no matter what he says. Then when his "enchantment" comes upon him, he reverses his argument. "It is at this hour that I am in my right mind: it is all the rest of the day that I am enchanted." How should the children know which to believe? Pause in your reading at the bottom of page 164, and again at the bottom of page 165, and finally after page 167, to ask yourself what you would do in the children's situation.

DISCUSS QUOTES

Explain the following quotations. What do they mean in context? What do you think of the ideas expressed?

- "You have seen lamps, and so you imagined a bigger and better lamp and called it the *sun.* You've seen cats, and now you want a bigger and better cat, and it's to be called a *lion.*" (the Witch, p. 180)

- "Friends . . . when once a man is launched on such an adventure as this, he must bid farewell to hopes and fears, otherwise death or deliverance will both come too late to save his honor and his reason." (Prince Rilian, p. 193)

JOURNAL WRITING: Write a Conversation

Since Aslan knows all that is to come, he must know that Jill will miss some of the signs. If that's true, why do you think he gives them to her? Why do you think he sends the children on this quest rather than simply freeing the Prince himself? Suppose you could talk to Aslan. What would you ask him about this? How do you think he would answer? Write this imagined conversation in your journal.

BOOK 7
THE LAST BATTLE
"The stars never lie, but Men and Beasts do. If Aslan were really coming to Narnia the sky would have foretold it." (p. 19)

SETTING THE SCENE
Narnia—where you must say good-bye—and where the adventure begins again.

A donkey in a lion skin is claimed to be the real Aslan and is used by figures far more powerful than he to control Narnia for their own ends. In despair, King Tirian calls to children from another world—children who always seem to come when Narnia is in trouble. It is up to the two who arrive—Jill and Eustace—to rescue the King from the Calormenes and expose the false Aslan. However, it is not easy for all of the Narnians to see who is real and who is false. And to some it makes no difference. The war leads to a victory other than the one the children expect: It leads to the end of Narnia, and to the beginning of another world.

QUESTIONS FOR GROUP DISCUSSION

• In the first chapter, which do you think is Shift's most clever argument in getting Puzzle to do something he doesn't want to, or something he knows he shouldn't? Why do you think Shift acts as he does?

• How are people and animals manipulated into believing in the false Aslan? How is the argument "He is not a *tame* lion" used? The Mouse says, "He seems to have come back very angry this time. . . . We must all have done something dreadfully wrong without knowing it." (p. 45) How does their sense of guilt make them more gullible?

• Characters frequently face the decision of when to act and when to wait. When is quick action helpful? When is it harmful? Find examples in the text.

- How does the symbol of the stable door operate? Why do you think it is bigger on the inside than on the outside?

- Who are the seven friends of Narnia? What has happened to the eighth, Susan? Why do you think the author reveals this information slowly?

- Explain the role of the Dwarfs in the story. How did they come to be so mistrustful? What do you think they mean by their refrain, "The Dwarfs are for the Dwarfs"? What happens to them on the other side of the stable door and why? Why can't they see what the others see?

- Explain the relationship between the Old Narnia, the world that is destroyed, and the world the narrator comes to call the "real Narnia."

- What happened to the children in their own world? Do you think this ending is sad? Why or why not?

THINKING ABOUT DIFFICULT QUESTIONS

What cultural, racial, and religious prejudices of the author's time and in history might be reflected in his attitude toward the dark-skinned Calormenes and their god, Tash?

The book has a strong negative answer to the question of whether Aslan and Tash are the same. Why do you think the answer is so strong?

DISCUSS QUOTES

Explain the following quotations. What do they mean in context? What do you think of the ideas expressed?

- "Their prison is only in their own minds, yet they are in that prison; and so afraid of being taken in that they cannot be taken out." (Aslan, p. 169)

- "All the service thou hast done to Tash, I account as service done to me." (Aslan, p. 188)

JOURNAL WRITING: Metaphor

"All their life in this world and all their adventures in Narnia had only been the cover and the title page: now at last they were beginning Chapter One of the Great Story which no one on earth has read: which goes on forever: in which every chapter is better than the one before." (pp. 210–1) Explain the metaphor the author chooses to end *The Chronicles of Narnia*. Why do you think he made this choice?